Quickies – 2
A Black Lace erotic short-story collection

Look out for our themed Wicked Words and Black Lace short-story collections:

Already Published: *Sex in the Office, Sex on Holiday, Sex in Uniform, Sex in the Kitchen, Sex on the Move, Sex and Music, Sex and Shopping, Sex in Public*

Published in May 07: *Sex with Strangers*

Published August 07: *Paranormal Erotica* (short-stories and fantasies)

Quickies – 2

A Black Lace erotic short-story collection

BLACKLACE

Black Lace books contain sexual fantasies.
In real life, always practise safe sex.

This edition published in 2007 by
Black Lace
Thames Wharf Studios
Rainville Road
London W6 9HA

Toys	© Stella Black
All I Have To Do	© Nikki Magennis
Gettysburg Undress	© Amber Leigh
Slow Burn	© Sophie Mouette
Sweet Charity	© Monica Belle
Missionary Impossible	© Maya Hess

Typeset by SetSystems Limited, Saffron Walden, Essex

Printed in the UK by CPI Bookmarque, Croydon, CR0 4TD

ISBN 978 0 352 34127 3

Toys Stella Black

'Stella. I told you. One toy only.'

'But I want the Ami Yumi doll and the Ami Yumi cat, what's the point of having one and not the other?'

'I told you. One toy only and if you argue with me I will take you into the car park, I will take your pants down and I will spank you. Do you understand me?'

I considered lying down in the middle of the corridor marked 'Action Toys' and remaining supine until he bought me exactly what I wanted. I am five foot three, after all, and eight stone. Petite in one sense, but difficult to move in the other. Still, even I, immersed in lovely fantasy as I was, recognised that a 23-year-old woman having a tantrum in the middle of the Toy Palace might cause more problems with the security department than was necessary. He was a kind Daddy, a good Daddy, a cruel Daddy, a perfect lover and role-player, but he would not be able to explain himself to the outside world. The outside world would not understand. But the outside world, at this moment, was of no importance. We had our world.

We were playing. He was hard and I was wet and it was bliss.

'But!'

I liked defying him but I knew it was risky. I knew that he meant it. I knew that if he became annoyed, if I overstepped the mark, he would tan my arse for me and it wouldn't be easy. He had a hard hand, and if he didn't feel like using that he used a Mason and Pearson hairbrush, or sometimes a paddle. It wasn't easy. I had the bruises to prove it.

But somehow, I never actually believed he would do it, he could do it, until he actually did it. And here in the Toy Palace, one of my favourite places by the way, here in the Toy Palace, amongst the Wheebles and Whoozits, he just looked like any other good-looking 32-year-old man in a dark coat.

The discerning eye would know that the coat was Gaultier. He did have money, a lot of it as it happened, he had inherited a fortune when he was 28, and he was prone to indulge himself as a result. He was a hedonist, but without the self-destruction that that sometimes implies. And now, he was my big Daddy. He loved it. I loved it. I was his naughty girl. We were free.

I gazed, lost in the biggest toy shop in the world. Well. That's what the sign said. It was what the Toy Palace believed. THE BIGGEST TOY SHOP IN THE WORLD. This meant a fantastic kingdom of plastic and wood and primary colours.

It meant that Barbie had a private jet and the Star Wars 'Republic Senator' had a snake-like tongue with which to threaten his enemies. There were Froggies and Doggies and Pony Rescue and Playmobil sniffer dogs all of which could be explored for hours on end.

I never became tired of it, though the Daddy sometimes became a little impatient and would take me hard by the hand and march me to the till where I was allowed just the one thing. Only one. Though no price limit! Well, even with that restriction. You try it. One toy in the biggest store in the world?

'I've spoiled you, Stella,' he would say. 'I've spoiled you, and I've created a bad girl.'

Rules were made to be broken. He made them, I broke them.

The rules said I was to be polite in the shop, not ask for things, not whine or sulk.

He took me by the hand and led me over to a large aisle entitled, 'Dressing Up!' Masks stared down at us. Fanged freaks, dragons, one-eyed zombies and scarred Nazis – a hideous gallery of imaginative prosthetics and sinister teeth. And on to the outfits. There was nothing you couldn't get. Your baby could be a monkey, a duckie or a pumpkin. Your son could be a fireman, a Bob the Builder, or a Dementor. The teenager could be a cool ghoul, a night slasher or a high seas rogue.

He dragged me past all this to the teenage girls section. If he makes me be a Tinkerbell I'll never speak to him again, I thought, though Skeleton Bride was good, as was Dragon Geisha and Zombie Cheerleader. My spirits rose.

'There are nuns,' I informed him.

'You're not being a nun,' he said. 'It's not Monty Python. Just stand there.'

A young man appeared. His face was not his advantage. Indeed, his face could easily have taken its place amongst the Halloween masks. He was wearing a green nylon uniform with 'Toy Palace' and a castle logo embroidered in red on his chest.

'I'm looking for a witch.'

The assistant didn't say, 'Aren't we all?' as I would have done, but displayed an expression as wide and dry as the Gobi desert.

'Over here, sir,' he said in the voice of Shaggy from *Scooby Doo*.

Daddy stroked the back of my neck and, over-powered by fatherliness and his smell and my compulsion to take him into me, I nearly cried.

'I don't want a bloody witch outfit,' I said. 'I want...'

The shop assistant, walking ahead, did not hear.

'Don't be rude,' he said calmly. 'We've got to get something for Suzanne's Halloween ball. I'm putting you in a black net skirt, thigh-high boots, seamed stockings and PVC pants. We're getting the skirt here – the boots and knickers you'll have to wait for and, I might add, I will be caning and buggering you when you are wearing them.'

I stared at him innocently. I knew this costume would look good with purple lipstick, dark eyes ... I knew I would flip myself over for him, let him push the net over my head and cane me, slashing onto the PVC until my flesh started to sweat inside it and I would grow wet into that pervy plastic fabric.

'I don't want the witch. I want the cat!'

I put some gum in my mouth, chewed it, stared defiantly at him for a couple of seconds and then walked off in the opposite direction, past shelves piled high with farm animals, past plush badgers, past mighty Action Men with inmate muscles and criminal leers.

I knew he would like the sight of my disappearing rear, little white Chanel shorts with a gold chain around the waist, Punky Fish jacket, Japanese teenager socks, Betty Page pumps, open toe, black velvet, high, with tiny polka dots and dear little bow on the back of the heel. They were the most adorable things you have ever seen, a mixture of pure pervert and adorable innocence that is very difficult to achieve in a shoe.

He loved them. Well. He should do. He had bought them.

The shoes were new. We had gone round the shops in his chauffeur-driven sedan, smoothing our way through Bond Street and Mayfair.

The peculiar boutique, hidden away in a mews, seemed to be designed for people like us. I expect he found it in a 'specialist' magazine. I hadn't realised there were so many of us around. I saw another Daddy with a naughty girl sitting on his lap, a beautiful Eurasian, mid-thirties, extending her foot to a kneeling assistant while her lover nuzzled her neck.

She walked up and down, showing him the little white boots. They were laced up to the knee of her bare brown legs and teamed with a pair of white culottes and a striped Paul Smith blazer. I thought they were marvellous but her daddy shook his head and said, 'No.' I swear she cried. I thought he was going to slap her but he kissed her on the mouth and pointed to a lovely pair of dark-green faux crocodile stilettos with four-inch heels.

We are around, naughty girls. We can do anything. And will.

My Daddy – not my real Daddy of course, he died years ago – my pretend Daddy indulged me and fucked me and spanked the arse off me when I was rude to him, or didn't present my cunt when he asked me to, and we had fun with our minds and mutual attraction. And his dick.

So off I went, away from him and his witches outfits, disappearing around the Mermadia Sea Butterflies, past Simpsons Monopoly and something that the Furbys had bred. Past a 'Winged Puffball', past a knight fighting a dragon with *jo lan* ninja martial moves, until I was lost in every sense, subsumed by thoughts, surrounded by animatronics. Then. Oh my God, Daleks. There they were, in every shape, size and form. Dalek pens, Dalek lunch boxes, remote-controlled Daleks, Dalek T-shirts, Dalek tins. Annihilate. Exterminate. Destroy. I felt a rush of genuine pleasure. Daleks have always made me feel very very happy.

You might ask, and it would be fair to do so, how the terrifying metal maniacs of Who lore infiltrated the psycho-sexuality of Ms Stella Black, unfettered tart of the perve parish? But there is a link between terror and safety and sex, my friends.

Deep in the memory cells of the parasympathetic nerve system there lurked old stories of omnipotent robots whose mission it was to destroy all; and somewhere out there there was a male person destined to protect me from them. At an age when Dr Who was God, and God was the Father I had no real Father, only a distant grave and a strange disappearing act and no explanations. There was a deep longing for a protector; a man who was easy to admire and before whom all enemies fell. A man whose style reflected self-confidence and insouciance and a mighty intelligence gathered from many planets over centuries of time travel.

My childhood, if it could be called that, was

an odd one. The early years were full of Cyber-men and Ice-Warriors and Yeti, all scaly and furry and whispering and scary. Somebody whom I could not remember put me to bed during those years. He was nice and he loved me and then he went. I searched and looked and prayed to the God the Father invented by some-body at school but he never came back and I faced the world alone. Now he was here in a different form. A form that understood me. And loved me. And played and played.

Of course I wondered whether I would marry my role Daddy, whether we would *end up together*, though I didn't fancy having to talk to his boring friends or explain myself. I didn't fancy silent breakfasts and the mundane detail of morbid domesticity. I mean I would have liked to have been engaged in a camp 1950s way. But, in the end, the sex was spectacular and absorb-ing and enough. We were distant but close. Our world was safe and sexual and imbued with complete trust and perfect understanding.

The best moments were lying slumped against each other in the back of a limo, smelling of the night's scents, some bar cigarettes, me Paloma Picasso, him Givenchy, warm, his hand playing me, making me wait for it, winding me up.

Men had bought me jewellery in the past; they didn't understand the toy fetish. I didn't really want jewellery, I always lost it anyway, I wanted love, as we all do, and I am cursed with wisdom. I know that love is more than a bling thing from Tiffany. I know it is about time and trust.

Daddy arrived in November, at a dance in an earl's mansion in Belgravia. I think I had fucked the earl once or twice in the past, in the Cap d'Antibes or somewhere. I was Roxy Music in vintage Anthony Price. Most of the men had dismissed me because I was cleverer than them. I got incredibly bored and went to explore the magnificent residence which was one of those places with an indoor pool, Ionic pillars and several original Chagals. Around the third floor I found a bathroom the size of an apartment with two marble sinks, gold mirrors and a free-standing bath adorned with a parade of Floris and Jo Malone.

Nobody would have been able to resist that and I did not. Off came the moire dress.

I was relaxing in delicious hot waves of geranium scent when he walked in. I was, of course, completely naked, though my modesty, such as it is, was protected, to an extent, by the high white walls of the Victorian bath.

He didn't say sorry. He hardly looked at me. He simply padded across the soft white carpet, pulled out his dick and went to the loo. I did not provide him with the gratification of staring at his organ, curious though I was, as one always is. Instinct told me that he was fine in that department. It's a talent I have. Assessing dick size by the reading of the personality. I am rarely wrong. I'll tell you how to do it sometime. It's quite useful.

He sat on the edge of the bath, lit up a cigarette and smiled at me through the smoke.

I soaped myself, particularly my breasts, which weren't particularly dirty, in the usual sense of the word. I looked at him straight in the eye and lathered between my legs. Then I stood up and rinsed myself with the shower, ensuring that he was allowed the full advantage of a rear view that, with thoughtful presentation, could cause a bus to crash into the back of a police car.

Finally, I lay back into the water, legs spread, toes on the edges, little crimson nails winking at him, little crimson lips slightly parted to reveal my clit.

He took his time but we both knew it was up to him to lead. The water nearly went cold. I'm not a patient person and neither do I sit in cold water for any man, even if he is one of the darkest and best looking I have ever seen. At last he stood up and gathered a vast white towel from the silver rails.

'Come to Daddy,' he said. 'It's time for bed.'

I was home.

We fucked for a fortnight before we found our mutual core. It was after a night of anal sex. It's a strange thing, anal sex. It always makes me feel violated and small and submissive. I have to be taken to it very slowly, and with some dominance. He quickly discovered that.

I was lying on my stomach on his bed, wearing a pair of pink cotton pants and matching socks and very little else. I was reading the *Beano* and eating sweets and being very Nabokov. I got some chocolate on his counterpane and he was furious.

'For God's sake, Stella,' he said. 'It's eighteenth-century silk. You can't dry clean it, it will destroy it.'

'Well, it's very stupid to have it on the bed then,' I responded, popping another candy into my mouth. 'Give it to the V and A or something.'

I turned the page to Dennis the Menace and Gnasher.

He didn't say anything. He simply took the *Beano* and the packet of sweets and placed them on the bedside table. Then he ambled over to the dressing table where, amongst a line of antique clothes brushes, there was a silver-backed hairbrush that had once belonged to an aged aunt.

He grabbed me, spread me over his knee, ripped down the Lolita knickers and beat me with that silver-backed brush.

The sound rang out as a slap into the room. God knows men have spanked me before. I seem to bring it out in them for some reason. But this took me by surprise as we had not discussed it. The stings became harder and my flesh hotter. I yelped. Then the erotic flush turned into red pain. He slapped my thighs and then returned to my arse, again and again, for about twenty minutes, until the arousal and discomfort melded and I eased smoothly into the true transcendence of total submission.

He went all the way, spanking me, fingering me, spanking me again until I wept and said, 'I'm sorry. I'm sorry. I won't do it again.'

My pants were then removed completely and his fingers, lubed with Vaseline, eased into my back passage.

'Play with yourself, Stella. I want you to relax.'

So I brought myself to orgasm as he fingered me slowly and did as I was told. For once.

He kissed me on the lips, and pushed me face down over the edge of the bed. I was kneeling on the floor, but my forehead was pressed into the aforementioned eighteenth-century silk.

He left me there for a minute or two, knowing that I love to wait for it. My smacked bottom was presented red and animal-like to him. My cunt was wet. And slowly, his dick wrapped in rubber, he eased himself into me. Very gently. In and further in. I was naked now, except for the knee socks, snivelling and moaning but turned on, allowing him through.

There was only me and him and his dick and my anus. Somewhere there were our smells and the smell of chocolate. I went somewhere, returned, went away again. He started to thrust harder, letting himself go and surrendering to his ejaculation.

Later, after smoked salmon sandwiches eaten naked, he tucked me underneath the white duvet. We were naked and together and close.

After that he took charge.

Once he made me stand outside the gates of a school yard wearing a St Mary's public school uniform. My dark hair was in bunches tied with pink plastic baubles. God. I even had a tight white shirt and a green and yellow striped tie. Very St Trinian's. Very me. I looked as if I had a whisky still in the science lab and a racehorse in the dormitory.

I was chewing gum and swaggering about with my satchel when he pulled up in the BMW.

Seeing him, I dropped the lipstick which I had been applying into a Hello Kitty compact mirror, bent down, and gave him the full vision of a round butt framed by a grey pleated skirt and barely covered with white cotton panties.

He wound down the window.

'Get in, Stella, and stop showing off.'

He drove to his flat in Knightsbridge. There was a grand drawing room with huge portraits of relations and a lot of tassels and upholstery. There was a statue of a horse and a bust of John Donne and several seriously valuable eighteenth-century banquettes. There was a woman painted by Reynolds and a grand piano made in

1820. It was like the John Soane Museum without the entrance fee.

Homework was a dry Martini and a blow job delivered with genuine affection. I liked to torture him with my mouth – I liked it when he nearly burst and just had to fuck me or he would die.

'Ladies and gentlemen, please note that the Toy Palace will close in ten minutes. Please make your way to the checkout area.'

I don't know how long I had been lost in aisles of Twinkleberries and plastic princesses.

Somehow my trolley had filled up with Daleks. I simply don't know how they got there, by themselves, probably, knowing them.

If he doesn't let me have these, I thought, I am going to pay for them myself. I'm not leaving this shop without a Dalek and that is all there is to it.

He was waiting at the till. The witch outfit was in a carrier bag.

I knew he was about to blow. It was my pleasure to press the button of that detonator. I love being annoying to men, I just do. I can't help it. But only with the men with whom I am in love – the others? I'm not interested in playing with them.

'Where have you been? I've told you about wandering off.'

'So get me a mobile. Or tether me or something...'

'Don't you dare speak to me like that!' He was furious. 'The more I give you the more you take.'

The last time he had been so cross we had been in Harrods and I had made him wait for more than ten minutes by a handbag counter. He hated waiting. Who doesn't? But he was rich enough not to have to queue for anything, and didn't. Everything was delivered. Tailors came to him. His assistant arranged things.

Anyway the time in Harrods he dragged me into the ladies' loo without taking any notice of the uniformed attendant, a plump woman in her mid-fifties. As she stared in silence at us, he bent me over the marble basin, lifted up my miniskirt, pulled down my pants and spanked me until I couldn't sit down for a week. I remember seeing my face in the mirror, over the gold taps, a picture of flushed cheeks and pain and then wishing he would stop because it was too much, but he went on and on, a real good smacking so that you knew you had been punished and you would feel the heat throughout your lower body for hours. And then wetness...

The attendant didn't bat an eyelid and calmly accepted a £50 tip.

Daddy had a huge erection and propelled me down the escalator and into the waiting car so quickly my feet hardly touched the ground. And bliss, over I went, over the back of the drawing-room sofa, knicks down, arse up, wet pussy, buttocks still red. Then his fingers in, him kissing me, dick in, filling me up. We came together in one of those rare moments of pure mutual understanding and physical release.

He pulled my hands away from the bars of the trolley where they were gripping so hard my knuckles had turned white. He didn't even look down at the Daleks, of which there were about twenty, and one of whose voice-activated mechanism was chanting in the familiar (and well-loved) tone of threat.

'Exterminate.'

'Exterminate.'

'Destroy.'

I smiled.

He glowered and his eyes flashed dangerously. 'I've had enough of you.'

'But . . .'

'No.'

'But I want . . .'

'No.'

'If you don't let me have a Dalek I am going to scream and it is very likely that you will be arrested.'

'If you utter another word, young lady, I will take down your pants and I will spank you here, on your bare bottom, with your shaved puss showing, and I will not stop until you beg me for mercy and perhaps not then . . .'

We faced each other in a sexual stand off, bluffing, seeing who had the nerve to go the furthest. It was usually me. He had a job, after all, with responsibilities and position. I am an ex-porn star. I could always go for it. My reputation and sales could only be enhanced by bad behaviour. Blimey. The biography alone had sold a million in America. *I Stella*. Hardback. Paperback. Lots of colour photographs. I'm very marketable, you see, being rampant and the holder of a 1.1 degree in philosopy. I can talk post-fem and Foucault and even the *TLS* likes me. Particularly after I slept with one of the (female) editors. Anyway, if I had been arrested my publisher would have been most gratified and would have assumed that I had hired a private publicist.

Daddy won. Well. I allowed him to win.

People stared as we exited and I was being told off.

Jim the chauffeur (navy uniform, gold buttons, peaked hat) was standing by the car in the car park smoking one of the Benson and Hedges cigarettes that his friend smuggled in from Belgium.

'Successful trip, sir?'

Daddy didn't say anything, but merely pulled me around to the bonnet of the sedan, pushed my head over it so that my face was down and my arse was raised towards him.

Jim ground his fag out with the sole of his immaculate black brogue and got in the driving seat where he watched through the window.

Daddy pulled my white shorts down. No knicks, bare arse, long socks, heels. He slapped my right buttock with the full force of his hard hand. There were no preliminaries, no more threats, no easing into it with erotic slaps – he just smacked hard. And then another on the left. I yelped.

'Ow!'

I didn't have time to assess the situation, to think about Jim watching us, or the risk of being seen. The pain seared into my arse and took all thoughts away.

Smack. Smack. Smack.

He hit me with the flat of his hand with all his strength for ten minutes. It was a hard spanking and I knew I had asked for it. He went on and on until he smelled and felt and heard my genuine supplication. I was wet and weeping and desperate for him. Ah me. There's nothing like romance.

'I'm sorry.'

He reached down and picked up the shorts, which were now on the ground. Then he hugged me and helped me gently into the back of the sedan where I lay with my head on his lap and my arse naked, hot and wet and tearful. He stroked my hair and kissed me.

Then he handed me the biggest Dalek of the

range. Radio controlled, twelve inches, flashing lights, automated head movement, poseable gun and arm, blast sound effects, authentic voice mechanisms and illuminated eye.

'You make your Daddy very very happy.'

Stella Black is the author of the Black Lace novels *Shameless* and *Stella Does Hollywood*. Her short stories have appeared in numerous Wicked Words collections. Her erotic memoir, *Daddy's Girl*, is published by Virgin Books in June 2007.

All I Have To Do

Nikki Magennis

Remember home-made mix cassettes? The ones that lovers used to make for each other, shyly choosing tracks that hinted at all their furtive desires without using the actual words. Songs that made you smile, made you swoon. A gift that you puzzled over, wondering if they really loved you or just wanted a little carnal adventure. One of those sweet little gestures that seems so innocent now, now we're all grown up and too tired for games.

I found one today. With my name on the outside in red pen. The songs listed on the paper insert, your writing small and scratchy.

I remember getting it, that day in June, so long ago. The parcel in the post arriving with a delicious thud on the doormat. Before I was fully awake. Sticky with sleep, I bolted to the door to find what well-wrapped present you'd sent, heart fizzing with nerves, as hopeful and desperate as a kid on their birthday. I remember everything about that summer, even the light. It was as though even the sunshine had its own particular yellowy scent, the dusty stones warmed by sudden light that seemed to break open the city and promise endless, sweet freedom. I was living on air and white wine then, full of a vivid energy that carried me through my crummy office job and sailed me quickly from weekend to weekend. Yes, it was like sailing. A sea full of light, insubstantial water, a huge open vista of parties and dancing and smiling young men, eyes glittering with that electric look that meant sex.

Everything was bright, and everything was moving so fast you couldn't touch the sides of your life. Dizzy. And in amongst the sweaty clubs and drunken grinding of a hundred lost weekends, I met you, with your white smile. Your chocolate-smooth voice. Your fine, long fingers and your delicate frame, built to craft melodies. I could tell from the way you moved the air around you that you were someone who created things. You seemed to promise something vast and expansive. We danced without speaking, lurching slowly round the slippery floor in that way that lovers do, trying to press body parts as close to each other as possible, feeling wonderful bulges that begged further exploration. Hanging round the dark corners, interlacing fingers in a gesture that means: as I push my hands into yours, so I will fuck you. On a wave of booze, lust and music, we swayed. Later, five in the morning, with the glow of dawn chilling us quietly, you sang to me.

The Everly Brothers. A song like honey, like being wrapped in sweetness. You held my wrist and stared into my palm, like you were looking for something. While my hungry young pussy was clamouring for attention, something in the way you sang reached deeper, turned even my heart into a puddle. After the song finished the room seemed changed, as though the low timbre of your voice had altered the world. Made a space. Wide with possibility, heavy with intent. More than fucking, your singing promised that I would be utterly explored, utterly turned on.

And then you were gone.

There were phone calls, and I'd tangle the phone cord round myself like I was wrapping myself in your voice, coiling it round my ankles and wriggling. Letting you tickle my ear with your laughter. Listening to the sounds in the background, the landscape of your life, so distant and alluring. You sent letters too, written in the same red pen, sheafs of creamy paper tucked in parcels that had the aura of relics, the sense of you folding them and slipping them inside like little secrets.

You were so far away, so unreal, that my whole body ached for you. I became super-sensitive, shivering at the sound of your voice at the end of the phone, as though you were touching me just by speaking. I pictured you moving around in your city, making songs in your room, trying out notes on your keyboard with those gentle fingertips, striking the keys with that suggestive weight, that playful touch. I wished so hard to feel you touch me that way that sometimes I felt the slightest bump against my neck or shoulder, as though some phantom hand of yours had reached out somehow across thousands of miles and made contact. I'd jump a little, and feel the warm tingling spread over me, like the liquid swell of post-orgasm. Like you'd turned your thoughts to me and made a mysterious, psychic fuck happen in my head.

Meanwhile, through my obsessive haze of your voice and words, I was hurtling through real life. I had the hysteric, vivacious hunger you get from losing something before you'd even got to play with it. I found a club that played soul, the songs so loud they warped the air and made the floor thud. I stuffed myself onto the inferno of the dance floor, squirmed through the tightly packed bodies till I found a boy with a cute face or a tight ass, thumped up against them and danced like a whore. The music was bottled sex, dirty and funky and delicious. You couldn't listen to it, only dance, and dance like you were coming right there on the crowded floor.

Shooting fish in a barrel. I'd always leave with a boy's arm draped over my shoulder, sometimes two. A trail of phone numbers was scrawled on hands, on beer mats, on flyers. Lipstick and eyeliner smudged the numbers – sometimes made up, sometimes real. And then there were hotel rooms, and foreigners. Sweat and body hair and tights with holes ripped in them. The kisses of starving people, so hard they made your head spin. Clothes shed like confetti, clumsy manoeuvres towards the bed, the shock and wonder of a strange tongue in your mouth, love bites tattooed down your neck. I loved that cocktail of tastes, the concentrated essence of men and decadence that was so heady and strong it was better than drugs. Almost addictive.

It got so easy to spread my legs for strangers I felt like a wild beast – a connoisseur of cocks and body hair, tasting their aftershave like vintage wine as they shoved their hands eagerly into my more-than-willing pussy.

Those brutish, fast and messy nights would leave me tender and satisfied, my body bruised like a piece of fruit and my skin all humming with the friction of men's hands, stubble, cocks. I'd wake on a Sunday morning and pass the day in a happy daze, the dirty sheets and hangover a glorious reminder of each new conquest. I'd lower myself into a scalding bath and let the water sting at my poor chafed parts. Relish the humming sensation of a body that's been well fucked.

In the evening, you'd call. The phone would ring gently like a cat meowing, and I'd pick it up carefully, take the receiver and hold it to my ear and receive your 'hello' like a kiss of benediction, a warm salve to wash away the night.

* * *

It was a slight, nothing-much of a love affair even in the beginning – both of us too shy to say anything blatant. A whole ocean to keep us apart. The more sweet and distant you got, the more wild and lascivious my weekends became. Booze, fellatio, cocaine, threesomes. One long summer of lust. I felt like that mythical woman the sailors used on long voyages – made of rubber; flexible; indestructible. And all along our chaste, dreamy conversations, little gifts, a longing that stretched out like aeroplane trails over the blue skies.

I racked up enough lovers to develop a kind of world-weary demeanour. Became so careless I didn't even try to remember their names, or cherish the battle scars. A skilled slut, I learnt how to lose people and how to enjoy even the slight ache of loss, the possible heartbreaks. I'd think with pride how my tits had been fondled by an army of men, enough almost to make up for the lack of you.

Time's passed, since then; the inevitable seasons come and go. I grew tired of debauchery and moved elsewhere. Your phone calls quietly stopped.

I got a house, a job. Took care of my lovely pussy and decided I would no longer hand it out to every cute guy I happened to dance with. After a long while, I hung up my dancing shoes altogether. I got a husband.

No more soul clubs, no more gut-vibrating beats to get my mojo going. No more long-distance phone calls and foreign parcels. No more love letters. Instead, I pay my bills and post thank-you letters. My hair got longer, and these days I wear less make-up. I still love fucking, but sex has become more comfort than dazzle. A way to knock ourselves out before sleep, grabbing for that pleasant buzz from each other like eating a slice of heavy cake. All those exotic and horny young men, left behind like my sweaty nightclub dancing clothes. Life built up around me like a piece of self-assembly furniture, surprisingly graceful as it fell into place. As I learnt how to be a human being. I watch the world pass now from behind large clean windows. I smile at the shopkeeper when I buy milk; I ignore his glittering eyes, the raised eyebrow. It seems you become immune to all the little signals, kind of dulled. As though there's a secret world of signals and scent and glances that gets left behind as you age, overtaken by more important languages. Subtler, saner conversations. All my friends got fat. We got money and started sagging at the edges.

Sundays these days I wake up with a clear head and take a walk in the park. I climb the hill and look down on the city, lying there like a vast jigsaw puzzle: mapped, tattered, understandably complicated.

I live within familiar patterns. Supermarket.

Kitchen. Chop spring onions with a matchstick in my mouth to stop the tears. Hoover. Wash. Consider the wall colours.

Still, no matter how organised my life is, I have shelves overflowing with junk, cupboards full of things that lurk in the dust and murmur to me. Make me feel guilty.

So this afternoon I started, gingerly, pulling open old boxes and sifting through the detritus. On my own in the bedroom, husband collapsed next door under the papers, I unfolded pieces of ancient history, touching them quietly so as not to disturb the patina of age, the weight of forgotten history. I found stashes of old love letters, cringeworthy teenage adulation spilling from the pages. The thousand lies of old boyfriends, recorded forever on blue onion-skin paper. Kneeling on the bedroom floor with the sisal rug making ribbed dents in my flesh, I got submerged in all the preserved pieces of time past. Stashes of photographs emerged. Pictures floated into my field of vision, images of a more colourful time. Those days I wore bright lipstick and listened to music so loud it infuriated all the neighbours. It was all brighter, harder, more desperate and more furious, days when you flung yourself into things. Your whole body. Your whole self.

I was lost in wry and pretty memories when I found that tape. Small and plain, it was a little bomb that set something off in me. All the blood rushed to my head and I felt my heartbeat pounding like I'd swallowed a clock.

Without making any more noise than I had to, I slipped it in my pocket and carried it into the study. Closing the door behind me, I walked straight to the Bang and Olufsen stereo and slid the tape in the slot. I settled in the big faux-leather chair and felt myself sink deep into the cushions. I put on the big padded earphones that smell faintly of aftershave. I pressed play.

There was a hissing noise, and it suggested the sound of that summer, the interference pattern that played as background music to all our coy telephone conversations. The sound of distance, of hunger and of unspoken, aching, aching longing.

When the piano chord struck, it hit me right in the chest, with a strong taste of bitter pleasure, like you'd laid your hand on me. That stereo is so perfectly tuned it seems that the music originates inside your own head, delivered straight to the most tender part of the mind. The part that responds instantly, overwhelmingly to sound. As though you were right next to me, close enough to touch.

And though the tape had lain untouched and silent for years it played with such ripe and vivid melody I could have wept.

Resonating, playing slowly up the scale, I felt your touch running over me again, fingertips brushing the side of my face as softly as new spring beech leaves. My lips were buzzing to feel you, to taste you. That lemon-tinged flavour of yours that echoed so faintly – I knew it was just on the edge of my tongue – then the song started, the words, and it was as though your voice was in my mouth, like a deep kiss. I might have expected to be moved – the bittersweet pang of long ago is one I'm accustomed to. What I hadn't counted on was that I'd be aroused. Eyes closed, I felt the song as much as heard it, felt your voice like silk over me, creeping into my ears and lulling me with those sweet words. 'Baby . . .' you crooned, and it was pure hell, pure hell and pure heaven all at once, as you insinuated yourself into my body all over again. I felt the lack of those lost days so strongly it hurt.

You sang about wrapping me in your arms, and I hugged myself, rocking, feeling at the same time the low beat of the drum bump along like you were bumping your hips against me, felt my nipples stiffen up as though you were nuzzling into my neck. I was leant back in the chair, the afternoon sun lying on my legs, warming me slowly, and the rest of the house started falling away, obscured by the lush and seductive sound of the music.

The strangest of feelings, being fucked by a song. My breath was heaving. Between my legs my cunt was undeniably buzzing, getting the slippery way it does when I'm anticipating sex. The desire was growing in me again, all the hazy, delicious desire of that long summer unfolding from within and multiplying like a psychedelic dream of pornographic detail. I felt myself swell and fall, my limbs grow heavy, my knees weaken. That wanton, reckless girl I dimly remember as my younger self seemed to awaken. The tug of sex stirred under my clothes, and I shifted in the chair. An old touchpaper was lit, burning quickly from my pussy and rising in my chest. I was sure that somehow I had grown young and juicy again, lips redder, tits magically prouder and as full as a bowl of fruit. I rubbed my thighs together, letting the crotch of my jeans agitate my clit. For once I felt mischievous, inflamed, vivacious again.

By now my clothes were all starting to itch and all I wanted was to strip and somehow bathe in that song, be naked in the sound and let it penetrate me, soak into my skin, pour into my ears and cunt. While you played, I could hear the deep breath you took before singing a line, and I swear I could feel a cold draught of air as you did so, your inhalation brushing over the back of my neck. With one finger I traced a line from my throat to my breasts, to the outline of my jutting nipples, crying out to be tweaked.

Just the way you would twang a guitar string, I flicked at myself, coaxing little shocks of pleasure from the hard tips. I pictured you doing it, with that half-smile of yours, the lazy lopsided way of looking at me with your head tilted and a splash of black hair over your eyes. When you wrote this, I thought, you were standing, one leg half bent to hold the guitar. Your hips angled forwards, and every note would send a vibration down the neck to shudder against your cock. I wondered at the thought of that sensation, the feel of the instrument between your legs, making you a little stiff, a little horny. At the image of your cock hardening, I let my legs spread wider, like you'd gripped my ankles and tugged them gently apart.

Was this what you'd wanted? When you wrote this song, were you imagining me lying back and slipping my hands down the front of my knickers? Was that low note you sang a way of courting me, like a songbird singing his mate into a state of readiness? Maybe you knew that the ache of this song would seduce me, maybe you wrote it with your cock in your hand while you imagined fucking me across oceans. Knowing that the notes would turn me liquid, would send me, writhing, on a voyage of erotic intent.

It was working. I was working on myself. One hand crawling inexorably down my belly towards my sex, my hips bucking in time to the suggestive drumbeat, biting my own lip to give it the stimulation of pain, if not the blessing of your warm skin.

It occurred to me that all the excesses of that summer might have been prompted by your innocent-sounding voice – the undercurrents of sexual want propelling me towards those dark basement clubs, into the arms of a different man every week. All the time I'd been enthusiastically sucking and writhing in the beds of strangers, I'd had the maddening want for you, for a night in your bed with you whispering dirty words in my ear. I worked my way through all those various cocks in a search for your elusive, beautiful presence. An echo of your melody-soaked possibility.

As I thought of this I was still pawing at the front of my pants, feeling the rough scratch of hair at the V of my thighs and knowing I had to bring myself off or go crazy listening to this heart-rending music.

A three-minute song wouldn't give me the drawn-out mindfuck I really craved and, realising I was halfway through the middle eight already, my dirty hands suddenly plunged right in, desperate to wring an orgasm out of this song, to come while you breathed a melody in my ears. It was burning heaven to feel fingers against my clit, frantic, hot as lava and as resounding as C major clanged out on a Steinway. Reviving. At the same time, I felt weirdly as though you were present, watching me, cheering me on with the rising chorus of your song. A performance as intimate and shocking as masturbating in public, and I felt my cheeks burn as though I were onstage, exposed as a slut yet unable to stop.

I rubbed that hungry pussy like I was strumming chords, loving the feel of it but still craving more. I felt the huge absence of your cock within me as I tensed my muscles. Panting, I rolled from side to side on the recliner in desperation to press myself against a firm surface, to feel friction, heat, the thud of satisfaction as the song rushed towards the climax. I knew it was foolish to think the bass beat was some priapic, rutting creature that had me impaled on its rhythm but believed it still in my delirium. Hanging on to your voice and the smooth growl of your lyrics, I spun myself tightly, thrusted upwards onto my hand and twisted, pressing, bringing at last and just in time a long, swooping rush of sweet gunfire hammering through my head and breaking open in a full-on orchestral clamour – you screamed, the last refrain, I moaned, I made a sound like I was breaking into tears as the guitars clanged, clanged, clanged. I came like a car crash, full speed and so hard I forgot to breathe for a minute, gasping, convulsing, curling over and letting the song carry me with it as it unravelled in a glorious, tangled crescendo.

And faded. I was holding tightly onto my pussy with one hand as the last chords softened and faded, a little reverb echoing sadly in the way one clings to a lover's neck, like the tide going out.

So I was left lying there like something washed up on the beach, flushed and mildly ashamed of my stolen tryst. How would one explain something like that? I just got fucked by a guitar, by a bass and a piano. True, what sent me spinning into lustful fantasy was mostly your honeyed voice, but in a way I felt I'd just wanked with a crowd of strange men as they played their instruments. Had a sordid fling with an imagined lover. Was this a common perversion? Teenage girls screaming at The Beatles, wetting their knickers with excitement. Kissing the pin-up posters on their bedroom walls. I felt like some obscene groupie as I pulled my clothes straight and let my heart thump out the last post-orgasmic beats. I'd given in to that old lust, the voracious appetite that used to send me spinning out to find a conquest. Still there, after so long. The desire for that pageant of sex. The fast motor of my libido had suddenly been jump-started so hard I was shocked by my own feelings. Like a wound-up teenage nymph, not a sober adult doing her Sunday housework.

The shakiness of afternoon sex made my movements uncertain, and I staggered to my feet with the headphones still attached, like a tethered animal, disoriented, suddenly come to from a lurid daydream.

It was when I turned to switch off the stereo, which was playing a hissing wail of white noise, that I realised I'd been caught. A shadow caught my eye.

Husband, hands in pockets, leaning against

the radiator. His eyes fixed on me, on my crumpled clothes and flushed face.

Awkward moments between a married couple are something to savour. When you've spent so long deep in each other's lives, breathing the same air, it's almost a gift to find yourself suddenly screaming with shame, humiliated in such a thoroughly shocking way. What did he see? Me writhing on the recliner, hands in pussy, face twisted in painful ecstasy, lips bitten. I searched wildly for an excuse, for a reason to explain why I was locked in rapturous union with the headphones, a thief caught red handed. Stealing a fuck from the distant past, committing adultery with my own memory. I was guilty as sin.

He could have left me hanging there, stewing in my own painful embarrassment while I tried to recompose myself. But it's at times like this when I realise one of the reasons I marched up the aisle with this man. One of the reasons I hang around and play house with him. Standing there, acres of space between us on that Sunday afternoon, he gifted me with one of those beautiful lopsided smiles of his. A splash of black hair in his eyes.

He traversed that vast space like it was nothing more than walking across the room. Pulled at my dishevelled clothes and laughed at me. With his voice like chocolate, like silk in my ear, he put his mouth to my ear and sang to me. It's always taken my breath away, how he forgives my lurid excesses with a shrug and a tease. How he can turn me on just by talking to me, but most especially by singing to me. Those Everly Brothers songs. When you sing 'Dream', it still turns my knees weak.

Nikki Megennis's short stories have appeared in numerous Wicked Words collections. She is also the author of the Black Lace novel, *Circus Excite*.

Gettysburg Undress
Amber Leigh

'Tomorrow we're going to rewrite history.'

Major General George Pickett raised his glass in the air to toast the impending victory. At his side, Major General 'Jeb' Stuart chuckled and plucked his cigar from the edge of the card table. Under plumes of smoke that hung listlessly in the billet tent, their laughter was a cacophony of vulgar mirth.

'What are you gentlemen plotting?' Vivien enquired.

Their table was a skirmish of maps and half-drained whiskey bottles. A souvenir mug, depicting the battle of Railroad Cut, had been conscripted for use as Jeb's ashtray. It overflowed with dead matches and the stubs of spent cheroots. Vivien knew the men took their re-enactments seriously – each year she encountered them at Olustee, Spotsylvania and this July pilgrimage to Gettysburg – but she couldn't understand why they recreated the squalor from the nineteenth century in their shared billet. The stench of cigar smoke clung to each breath like a greasy stain. The perfume of sour mash whiskey reminded her of spoiled fruit. With the rumpled sheets that covered their respective cots, and the clutter of anachronistic suitcases stuffed in one corner, Vivien thought Pickett and Stuart were as untidy as the messiest frat boys she had ever encountered.

Ignoring the disarray of their quarters she pouted at them. 'I thought one of you fine gentlemen was escorting me to the dance this evening. I saved this bodice and crinoline especially for tonight.' To show them how special the dress was she gave a brief twirl, displaying the gathers of vermilion silk, white velvet trim and the delicate decoration of dainty blue bows. The colours glistened like kaleidoscopic waves beneath the glimmer of the tent's lamps. The gown was cut tight to emphasise her slender waist and the bodice's plunging neckline gave the illusion that she had a magnificent bosom. Vivien had hoped the finished effect was appropriate for the period and might help her catch the eye of a general or two at the re-enactor's camp dance. Seeing the approving glint in George and Jeb's smiles, Vivien realised she looked as good as she had hoped.

But she could also sense they were more preoccupied with plotting mischief rather than paying her the attention she deserved. Their apparent lack of interest was a challenge and she silently vowed to make them take notice.

Throwing her shoulders back and pushing her chest out, she flicked her hair over her shoulders and graced them with her most alluring smile.

'Come and sit with us awhile, Miss Vivien,' George suggested. He shifted slightly on his bench and waited until Jeb had also moved so that there was a space between them. A devilish twinkle glinted in George's eye as he patted the slender seat and Vivien allowed herself the hope that she had already sparked his arousal. 'I'd love to impress you with an insight into my military genius,' George confided.

His comment dashed Vivien's hope that he might harbour an amorous interest and she turned her winsome glance in Jeb's direction. She was dismayed to hear the second officer expand on Pickett's claim. 'We're going to win the war for the Confederacy tomorrow,' Jeb promised. 'You'll be overwhelmed by our audacity.'

Although they weren't showing her the attention she wanted to enjoy, Vivien had to admit she was intrigued. Conceding she could miss the opening of the re-enactor's camp dance, she gathered the folds of her dress and stepped daintily across the groundsheet to sit between them. 'You're planning to win tomorrow's battle? I thought you were scheduled to lose.'

'That's what the organisers think too,' George said ominously. 'A lot of the spectators might be very surprised by how things turn out

tomorrow.' He chuckled and Jeb cheerfully echoed his merriment.

For all their faults in housekeeping, Vivien
could see George and Jeb had made scrupulous
preparations about their appearance. George had
grown his facial hair so that it properly resem-
bled Pickett's resplendent goatee and soup-
strainer moustache. He wore a double-breasted
frock coat cut from pattern grey serge. The outfit
was trimmed with the collar badge and cuffs of
an esteemed Major General. Shiny gold buttons
sat in twin rows of three against his broad chest
and torso. They sparkled brightly beneath the
dull glow of the tent's lamp and Vivien was
struck by the urge to touch them – tease one or
two of the buttons open – and dishevel Pickett's
otherwise meticulous appearance. Blushing at
the impropriety of that thought, shocked that
she could so easily find herself yearning for any
man in uniform, Vivien turned away.

She caught Jeb leering at her cleavage.

A knot of arousal tightened in her stomach.
Her cheeks blushed with a warmth that had
little to do with the balmy heat of the July night.
Between her legs her cleft was suddenly moist
with fetid excitement. The air in the tent thick-
ened with expectation.

She knew George and Jeb were probably not
their real names – the most ardent devotees of
the re-enactments got into character early in
the event and stayed that way until they were

heading home in their SUVs – but Vivien couldn't bring herself to break the magical atmosphere by asking either of them for their real identities. To discover that George was a CPA, or that Jeb sold surgical appliances, would shatter the world of illusion that had been created at the re-enactment.

Jeb, like George, had gone to excessive lengths to impersonate his hero. From the feather in his hat; through his full and flowing beard; over his frock coat; and down to his black leather boots: he looked every inch the dashing cavalryman Vivien had admired in a hundred or more history books. A sabre hung from the gold sash at his waist and his bulky yellow leather gauntlets drooped from one corner of the cluttered table.

Of the two officers, Vivien thought Jeb the more handsome and she met his gaze with an encouraging smile. If they had been alone she would have daringly toyed with the decorative tassels that adorned his sash. It would have been bold and suggestive behaviour – obscenely inappropriate for a well-mannered nineteenth-century lady – but it would have left him with no doubt about the urges that he stirred inside her.

'I'm not pressing too close against you am I, Miss Vivien?' Jeb asked courteously.

The bench they shared was barely big enough for two and she had been forced to squeeze between Pickett and Stuart. Thankful that her crinoline was made full by layers of petticoats and underskirts, rather than an inflexible whale-bone skeleton, Vivien smoothed down the silk of her dress and shook her head. 'I wouldn't complain no matter how hard you wanted to press against me, Major Stuart.'

His smile shone brightly through the flaxen forest of his moustache and beard. Slipping one hand beneath the card table he touched her thigh and murmured, 'I might have cause to remind you of that comment later on.'

The weight of his fingers against her leg inspired a sudden and glorious thrill. Vivien drew a sharp breath, not certain how to respond but sure she should say something suggestive.

George chose that moment to point at the map and ask, 'Are you familiar with what should happen tomorrow?'

Reluctantly, Vivien passed her attention back to Pickett and frowned as she tried to remember the schedule of events for the forthcoming day. She took a deep breath to distance her thoughts from the excitement Jeb inspired and turned her mind to the more mundane matters of the following day's itinerary. There was going to be a demonstration of nineteenth-century field surgery in Tent One, competing against a display of period fashions in Tent Two. She had already made up her mind about which of these she would be patronising but she didn't think George was referring to anything as commonplace as the listings for the re-enactment sideshows.

'You're going to lead a charge against General Henry Hunt's forces as they defend Cemetery Hill.'

It was an effort to keep her attention away from Jeb and she was thankful his hand continued to rest on her thigh. Admittedly, it was difficult to feel his touch through all the layers of stiff cotton underclothes but the movement of his fingers was comforting and made her believe her interest in the two officers was partially reciprocated.

'Pickett's Charge was a decisive moment at the battle of Gettysburg,' Vivien continued. She measured each word, scared of exposing the arousal that might rasp from the back of her throat. 'The troops were disciplined, resplendent and fresh for the fight. But they were attacking from an inferior position. They bravely went on to suffer decimation because of Lee's ill-conceived tactic to march through the centre of strong defensive forces. The history books repeatedly refer to Pickett's Charge as the high-water mark of the Confederacy.'

'You know your history,' George said with a smile. With a burst of Southern panache that made her feel weak he said, 'You clearly are as intelligent as you are desirable, Miss Vivien. You do Major Stuart and I a singular honour with your presence in our humble billet.'

Vivien placed a hand over her breast and coyly fluttered her eyelashes. 'Major Pickett,' she gasped coquettishly. 'I do believe you're flirting with me.'

To her left, Jeb squeezed Vivien's thigh. He made the pressure of his fingers firm against the taut muscle and brushed his bushy beard close to her ear. The scrub tickled gently against her cheek. His breath was a soft breeze that moved the tiny, delicate hairs at the nape of her neck. 'Pay careful attention, Miss Vivien,' he warned. 'You might discover that both of us are flirting with you.'

She swallowed thickly, aware that the atmosphere in the room was now heady with anticipation. Shifting her gaze from one officer to the other, her smile grew broader as she caught their lewd expressions. Glancing meaningfully at the whiskey bottle, she waited until one of them had poured her a generous shot of bourbon before thanking them both and asking, 'So, what is it that you boys are planning?'

'Major Stuart and I work well together,' George told her.

His fingers lingered against hers as he passed the tumbler. Tilting his face down, and contemplating her through hooded eyes, he traced gentle whorls against the back of her hand. Each feather-light caress made her more aware of how much she wanted the two officers.

'Would you care to see how well we work together?'

She swallowed again, amazed by her own

sense of daring. As George was touching her hand, and treating her to his smouldering appraisal, Jeb continued to stroke her thigh. She didn't let either know what the other was doing – a part of her suspected they were each aware of the other's actions – but she felt superbly decadent for dallying so intimately with the pair. Delicious spurts of arousal tingled through her body making her feel fresh, alive and excited. The heat inside the tent was suddenly stifling. Although she adored the elegance of her period clothes, Vivien now cursed the garments for being too cumbersome, tight and restrictive. It was difficult to draw breath because of the bodice and her nipples ached as they grew swollen and hard inside their confines. Squirming against her seat, and succumbing to another rush of giddy excitement, she wondered if Cemetery Hill was the only conquest the two officers were plotting.

'As you so rightly pointed out,' George continued, 'according to the event's organisers, my forces should be vanquished tomorrow.' His Virginia drawl was a smooth and genteel lilt. His mesmerising gaze never left her eyes as his fingers continued to caress the back of her hand. The tiny circles he described made her want to shiver with wanton desire. 'But, unknown to the organisers, Jeb and I plan to revise our battle plans. Tomorrow, the Confederacy will be victorious.'

Vivien finally drew her hand away and

snatched a sip from her glass of bourbon. The liquid burned her throat and stomach. Its syrupy taste filled her with a fire of excitement that complemented her mood. 'Stop teasing,' she protested. With an attempt at faux ignorance, playing on her role as a young debutante limited by a nineteenth-century education, she said, 'Remember: I'm just a simple girl. Tell me what you boys are plotting in a language I can understand.'

'We work well together,' Jeb explained.

Vivien couldn't tear her gaze from Pickett's hypnotic smile. She tilted her head, so that Jeb knew she was listening to him, but she couldn't shift her attention away from George. Unable to resist the impulse any longer, she leaned close to him and teased open one of the shiny buttons from the collar of his frock coat. He smiled for her and, seeing the lascivious gleam in his eye, she giggled and teased open two more. Her long slender fingers made light work of slipping the large brass circles through their respective slits.

'While Major Pickett is making his frontal assault, I'm going to be attacking the left flank,' Jeb explained.

Under other circumstances it would have been a bland remark. But, because one of his hands was evoking a delicious magic at her thigh and his other now stroked against her backside, Vivien didn't think there was anything dull about the comment. She drew a heavy breath and sipped a little more from her glass. Her body was charged with electric anticipation and she felt torn by indecision as she tried to decide which of them deserved her favours.

'Are you with us so far?' Jeb asked.

'Is this explanation clear enough for you, Miss Vivien?'

Not listening, she nodded blithely and begged them to continue.

While she had been delighted with the appearance of her crinoline, she now silently cursed its impracticalities. If she had dressed in anything other than the cumbersome dress she knew she would have properly felt Jeb's hand as it slid over her left flank. The idea of enjoying that sensation made her ill with the need to experience more. She crushed her thighs together, savouring the comfort that the pressure almost gave, while wishing the sensation was more profound. And, all the time, she continued to wallow in the thrill of Pickett's piercing gaze.

'Rather than trying to press through the centre of the Hunt's defences,' George said slowly, 'I'm going to take advantage of the weakness that Major Stuart will cause. I'm going to lead my troops through the confused forces on the left flank and, tomorrow afternoon, Pickett's Charge will be a success.'

She nodded, not sure she had heard a word spoken by either of the officers. Vivien had always loved the theatrical splendour of the re-enactments. Some went to the events for the sense of history. Others, she knew, appreciated the chance to sample a simpler period of history when the world didn't revolve around mobile phones, cars, computers and TVs. But, for Vivien, it was the sight of men in military uniforms that made her such a devotee: their elegance left her hot and breathless.

Being close to exquisitely tailored officers was enough of a thrill to have her inner thighs sweltering. It was also enough of a distraction to make her concentration glide easily away from whatever explanation George and Jeb had been giving. 'I'm sorry,' she mumbled. 'I didn't fully follow your battle plans for tomorrow. Can you show me?'

She sipped the last drops of her whiskey and glanced pointedly at the map on the cluttered table. Gettysburg was a complicated conflict to follow at the best of times. The key locations included Cemetery Hill, Cemetery Ridge and Seminary Ridge and Vivien knew those similar sounding names would have been enough to confuse her without the distraction of George and Jeb's lascivious attention. She believed, if they pointed out their intended manoeuvres on a map, she would have a better understanding of how they intended to win.

Jeb gallantly plucked the tumbler from her fingers and poured another shot of bourbon. Its smell no longer made her think of spoiled fruit.

Now that it was adding to the warmth inside her, Vivien thought the strong bouquet was a fiery aphrodisiac.

'Major Stuart and I can do better than show you,' George promised. 'If you'd be willing to indulge us, we can give you a practical demonstration.'

From behind her, with his large hands on her hips, Jeb helped Vivien to stand away from the bench. She felt momentarily intimidated by the two men but another quick swallow of the bourbon helped drown that sensation. George instructed her to stand in the centre of the tent with her hands above her head. It was a conspicuous pose and made Vivien fearful that the strapless bodice might not be able to contain her breasts if she kept her arms held too high for too long. Jeb remained behind her but he kept himself close and there was never a moment when she wasn't aware of his body pressing against hers. If not for the bulky petticoats beneath her crinoline Vivien believed she would have felt the thrust of his erection against her buttocks. The idea left her swathed in an unladylike sheen of perspiration. Trapped between the pair, and sure she now understood how they wanted the evening to progress, Vivien didn't allow any of her expectations to show on her face.

'I want you to imagine you're our intended target,' George began.

Vivien nodded. She privately believed her

imagination could be used for much more fertile devices – like the cause of the bulge that pushed at the front of Pickett's frock coat – but she didn't want either officer to know that her thoughts were descending to such lewd depths. Trying to show that she understood the demonstration, Vivien said, 'I'm your intended target.'

George grinned at her. 'I'm expected to make a frontal assault,' he explained. As he said the words his hands went to her breasts. The swollen orbs were barely contained inside her bodice. The tight garment almost pushed them over the plunging neckline. His cool fingers slid against the soft, pliant flesh and she bit back a sigh of delight as he gently kneaded her. The heels of his palms pushed against her bodice and excited the nipples beneath. Gently, but firmly, Pickett crushed them and inspired a poignant flurry of responses.

A stream of objections sprang to the forefront of her mind.

She thought of telling Pickett that he had misjudged her character; that he was overstepping the marks of decency; and that she wasn't such easy prey. But, before she could think of which argument to raise, Jeb's hands had fallen to her rear.

'I'm attacking the target from behind,' he explained.

His voice was disturbingly close. The whisper-soft caress of his words trailed against her neck and thrilled her with his nearness. It had felt like the height of audacity when George stroked her hand while Jeb touched her thigh. Now, to have one of them fondling her breasts as the other caressed her buttocks felt like the most decadent scenario imaginable.

Jeb had unfastened the lace ribbons that secured the back of her crinoline. She watched the glorious fabric pool to the groundsheet as he fumbled with the strings that tied her petticoats and bloomers in place.

'Major Pickett . . .' she sighed.

She swallowed, shook her head and started again.

'Major Stuart . . .'

George silenced her with a kiss. His beard and moustache tickled but the nuisance of that sensation was easily forgotten as his tongue slipped between her lips. While plundering her mouth, he continued to squeeze and caress her breasts until she felt the abrasive tear of her nipples being liberated from her bodice.

Vivien and George gasped in unison.

Exposed to the smoky air of the tent, her bare breasts looked small, pale and vulnerable. The tips were dark cherries, rigid and ripe against her porcelain flesh. Their sensitive ends were grazed against the coarse weave of George's dashing, grey frock coat.

'I think you've been undone, Miss Vivien,' Pickett said with a grin.

She didn't let him say anything else, pushing her mouth over his and stealing another deep kiss.

Jeb pressed behind her, easing layer after layer of petticoats away from her hips. Vivien only realised how many clothes he had removed when her legs and buttocks were chilled by the tent's cool air. Moving her lips from Pickett's face, she turned to glance at Jeb. His grin shone through the curls of his beard and, when she glanced down at herself, she could see her buttocks and thighs were exposed to him. An unsettled inner voice told her that there was too much of her flesh on display and she couldn't deny that the sight contrasted starkly with the ostentatious costumes of Pickett and Stuart. Seeing her predicament as though at a distance, she felt ill with arousal and had to bite back a sudden need to moan.

'Do you see how easily we can claim our victory?' Jeb asked. The tips of his fingers caressed her bare backside. Each revolution seemed to make him grow bolder as he inched closer to the crease between her cheeks.

'Or would you care for a fuller demonstration?' Pickett suggested.

Mute with anticipation – not trusting herself to speak – Vivien could only nod her consent. She allowed George to back away from her; kept her hands above her head while he admired her near-naked body; and stood motionless as they each murmured encouraging words about the spectacle she presented. When they finally moved to take her, she was weak with need.

'I will attack from the front,' Pickett reminded her.

He spoke as he lowered his mouth to her breast. Her left nipple was caught between moist lips, forcefully suckled, and then lightly nibbled. The balance of pleasure and pain swayed from one extreme to another. Her breast was a shriek of delicious responses in one moment and a bliss of punishing agony the next. When he shifted his mouth to her right breast, and treated her to the same cruel delight, Vivien knew she was already on the verge of climax.

Jeb's whisper-soft voice came from behind. 'I'm attacking from the rear,' he confided. The fingertips that had been chasing lazy circles against her rear became more inquisitive. His touch delved into the crease between her cheeks and she was shocked to feel him stretch her buttocks wide apart. It was too much – too intrusive – and she was about to tell him as much when he stroked the ring of her anus.

A quiver of raw ecstasy rippled through her body.

She gasped: disgusted and delighted.

Before she could catch her breath – and not sure if she wanted to tell him to stop or continue – George was teasing his fingers through the curls of her pubic mound. Every nerve in her body was charged with an adrenalin rush and Vivien shook her head from side to side. Her face blushed scarlet as she tried to work out if she should push herself towards Pickett or into Stuart.

George said, 'We're going to make it a forceful attack.' He spoke as his fingers slipped against the dank wetness of her labia. Deftly, he teased her pussy lips apart and drew a slow caress against the pulse of her clitoris.

'Our target won't know which side to defend,' Jeb assured her. His fingers remained at her rear, spreading her buttocks until she felt at her limit, and constantly exciting her puckered ring.

'We work well together,' George explained needlessly. He caught her clitoris between his finger and thumb and idly toyed with the pulsing bead of flesh. 'Tomorrow, we will rewrite history. Tomorrow, we will be victorious.'

Vivien didn't know whether they would be victorious on the battlefield but she knew they had triumphed over her. Overwhelmed by a need for satisfaction, she pushed herself into George's embrace. He guided her towards the cot, all the time teasing her between the legs while occasionally licking or sucking at her breasts. Jeb remained in constant contact with her behind, never letting his fingers lose their hold on her rear, and perpetually trying to ease a finger into her forbidden hole.

She had seen a hundred or more re-enactments,

and knew they could be fast and furious affairs. But she didn't think they would ever be as fast or as furious as the way she capitulated to the two Confederate majors. Pulling the hems of George's frock coat aside, tearing the erection from the front of his pants, Vivien impaled herself on him with a warm, liquid rush. His length was fat enough to spread her pussy lips apart and, as he slid into her sex, they both groaned with guttural cries of satisfaction. Her bare thighs were wrapped around his serge-covered hips. She smiled down at the elegantly dressed officer fondling her breasts and began to buck her pelvis back and forth. The pressure of his hardness rubbed beautifully against her pulse and she believed, with only a little more movement, she could secure the climax her body now needed.

Behind her, still practising his assault on her flank, Jeb pressed a rigid erection between her buttocks. Vivien was made momentarily ill when she realised what he was trying to do. And then her revulsion was swept away by a rising surge of arousal. The muscle of her sphincter offered the briefest resistance – she quietly fretted that shaft would be too large to enter the tiny hole of her anus – and then Stuart slid easily inside.

All three of them groaned.

Pressed between their uniformed bodies, delighting in the sensation of her own nudity being trapped between such an elegantly dressed pair, Vivien knew it would not be long before she heard the first canon-fire explosions of her climax. She remembered them both saying they worked well together and she now understood that they hadn't been lying. As Jeb thrust himself deep into her rear, George pulled his hips backwards and allowed his cohort to make the penetration without causing undue pain. As George shifted his hips forwards, filling her with his glorious, thick length, Jeb retreated until she fretted that his length might slip completely from her rear. They executed each lunge with practised precision, never allowing Vivien a moment when she wasn't fully impaled on one or the other. Jeb tried to cup her breasts as George continued to fondle her, giving Vivien the impression that she was being mauled by an entire platoon.

And then they increased their speed.

The pair slid easily in and out of her. Jeb pressed kisses against her neck and shoulders and rode his shaft deep into her bottom. George remained buried in her sex easing himself backwards and forwards with the pace of a quick march. The smoky stench of the tent was now lost beneath the scents of sexual musk, sweat and excitement. Vivien could hear both her holes squelching greedily although the sounds were almost lost beneath her faltering cries of delight. Pushed closer and closer to the pique of orgasm, while reaching behind herself to grip Jeb and pushing one hand down to hold George, she revelled in the moment of release as she stroked their debonair uniforms.

Jeb's climax quickly followed: squeezed from his length by the contractions of her inner muscles. His pulse came thick and fast, filling her with a molten seed that was so hot it inspired a blistering orgasm. She wrenched herself away from him, crying out with delight, as George erupted into her sex.

In the stillness of the aftermath, the three of them lay panting and satisfied together on the cot. Jeb was the first to move, tactfully withdrawing from the melee and quickly adjusting his clothes so he once again looked respectable. Vivien eased herself from George's recumbent body, smiling demurely for him as she began to retrieve her clothes.

He graced her with an approving smile.

'That was quite a demonstration,' Vivien murmured as she climbed back into her dress. Her body remained ablaze with excitement but she could see both officers were now spent and of no more use to her. Jeb gallantly helped her to fasten the bows and laces that secured her petticoats and crinoline but he performed the actions without any hint of his earlier attempts at seduction. Still breathless from the sudden burst of passion, and sure she could endure another clash with the pair, she fluttered her lashes from Jeb to George and asked, 'Will I see either of you at the dance later on?'

George was sitting up on the cot. He had put his spent length back in his pants and refastened those few buttons she had opened. As before, he looked like the epitome of uniformed perfection. 'We want to go over our plans again before we retire for the evening,' he said tactfully. 'But, if we're confident we know what we're doing before the end of the dance, you'll be sure to see us there, Miss Vivien.'

Understanding that she would see neither before their battle, Vivien graced each of them with a perfunctory kiss, thanked them and then left their tent. Her heart continued to race as she stumbled from their billet towards the sound of jaunty string music in the dance tent. Purple twilight flooded the sky, an end to the day as satisfying as the time she had just enjoyed with Pickett and Stuart. Vivien thought that bedding two high-ranking officers of the Confederacy – both of them resplendent in their full military regalia – was a fantasy made real. She was still smiling at the memory, and shivering with after-echoes of the pleasure, as she entered the dance tent.

'Do you have an escort for this evening, ma'am?'

She glanced up at the golden-haired officer, taking in the flowing curls that bounced against his shoulders and the dapper cut of his navy-blue uniform. The polished length of his shiny sabre glistened and, with a rush of mounting excitement, Vivien quickly caught her breath. 'General Custer?'

'At your service.' He bowed gallantly.

Bolder than she would ever have imagined herself, Vivien placed a hand against his broad chest. The weave of the navy cloth was deliciously coarse beneath her fingers. The coolness of the buttons was icy against her sweaty hands. She swallowed thickly as she saw his eyebrows rise with his expectation. 'I hope you truly are at my service, General,' she whispered. 'I've just heard two Confederate officers explain how they plan to cause havoc at tomorrow's re-enactment by making Pickett's Charge a success.'

Custer's eyes grew wide. For an instant Vivien sensed a real danger that the dashing young cavalry officer might briefly forget his character. 'Are you serious?' he gasped. 'Who are they? Why on earth are they going to do that? And how the hell could they possibly manage it?'

She glanced over Custer's shoulder and saw General Henry Hunt standing by the side of the dance floor with a drink in his hand and an affable smile twinkling through his beard. Although he wasn't as handsome as Custer, he looked resplendent in his military best and Vivien was won over by the sight of the Union uniform, dashing sabre and the splendid glitter of stars that adorned his epaulettes and cuffs. 'I can't tell you their names,' she began. 'That would be inappropriate. And I don't know why they're going to do it,' she added honestly. 'I never thought to ask.'

With obvious impatience, Custer asked, 'Can you tell me how they plan to do it?'

A sly smile graced her lips. Standing on tiptoe, pressing her body against his as she whispered in his ear, Vivien said, 'General Hunt should be with us when I tell you what they're planning. If you can find a discreet place for the three of us to discuss this matter, I will gladly demonstrate how they plan to be victorious.'

Amber Leigh's short stories have appeared in the Wicked Words collections *Sex in Uniform* and *Sex in the Sportsclub*.

Slow Burn Sophie Mouette

Karen gazed out through her powerful binoculars, scanning the familiar vista of pine-forested mountains, the needles dusty and tired-looking now with late summer drought. Following her long-established routine, she peered in every direction, looking for any telltale sign of fire: a plume of smoke, a flicker of flame, even unusual activity among birds and animals that might signal flight from a blaze not yet visible from the tower.

And in one direction, she watched for another telltale signal – a Forest Service vehicle heading for the base of the trail to the fire tower. The final approach was accessible only on foot, but David would bring his Jeep in as far as it would go and she would help him carry in the supplies he'd need for his shift in the tower.

David – her relief in more than one sense of the word.

At last, she saw the vehicle in the distance, its green and brown tones blending in well with the scenery. At this distance, she couldn't see much of the driver, but she filled in the details from memory.

Short-cropped fair hair. Dark eyes in a weathered face. Great legs that she'd first noticed in the shorts of his summer uniform. Long hands, strong and rough from outdoor work, but amazingly deft at touching her most sensitive areas. Cheekbones that suggested Scandinavian ancestry, although she'd never asked.

There were a lot of things she'd never asked David, a lot of things he'd never asked her. She wasn't even sure where he lived – they had each other's contact information but never sought each other out in town on the rare occasion they'd had off-duty shifts at the same time. Their relationship was here, in the fire tower, as one relieved the other for a six-month stint in the majestic solitude of the mountains. It worked for both of them.

Until now. This would be their last meeting here. The tower would be decommissioned after David's stint, replaced with aerial and satellite surveillance. At the end of the last shift, several rangers would come in to help carry out equipment and supplies that would no longer be needed.

And after that, who knows what happens to two hermits without a hermitage?

She set down the binoculars and began to make herself ready. Not that David expected a Victoria's Secret model waiting for him, but Karen enjoyed the occasional moments of not being her usual low-maintenance self.

She'd washed her hair the night before; even

in summer, the thick chestnut locks took a long time to dry in her usual tight braid. But her morning's routine had left her a little sweaty so she climbed down the one-hundred-and-twenty steps to the little living cabin and its solar shower stall.

This was her notion of luxury, one she would miss back in so-called civilisation: dappled sun playing on her bare skin as she soaped up, a pair of jays squabbling in a nearby treetop for music. She was hyper-aware of the flow of soap and sun-warmed water over her skin.

For days at a time out here, she could forget she was a sexual being. Sensual, yes, revelling in sun and rain and the play of light, pine fragrance and bird call and simple tasty food. Sexual, no. Now she was letting herself remember.

She imagined David's hands on her slippery body, sliding from her shoulders down her torso and back to her breasts. As she imagined, she echoed her fantasy with her own hands. Her nipples tightened. Blood seemed to pool in her groin, changing her centre of gravity, making her feel weighty and languid.

She was tempted to slip a hand between her thighs, but she didn't have time for that. The downside to solar showers was that there was only so much time to linger.

She finished rinsing just in time.

She patted some of the water off then headed, naked and damp, into the cabin.

The ten-by-twelve interior was spartan: a narrow bed topped with a sleeping bag, a plastic chest of drawers, a plain pine wardrobe, a folding table and camp chair, Coleman stove and lantern. Shelves on the walls held a curious but organised mix of canned and dried food, books, first-aid supplies and other necessities. But a bunch of wild flowers filled a salsa jar on the table and the table itself had a bright purple tablecloth.

She had other little luxuries squirrelled away as well.

From a mostly emptied drawer that had until recently been full of cotton panties and hiking socks, she pulled an emerald-green stretch lace camisole and matching boy shorts. She slipped into the lingerie and checked the effect in the scrap of a mirror, stretching and turning so she could get a better idea. She'd tried them on in her apartment when they'd first arrived, but that had been months ago.

They still looked good. If she wanted to be critical, the classic Forest Service tan − face, forearms, a V at the neckline and a bit on the legs − didn't complement the outfit, but she wasn't in the mood to be critical.

David would be there soon, and his Forest Service tan and hers would be wrapped together. That was all that mattered.

She put a clean uniform on over the lingerie. eCrisp short-sleeved tan button-down shirt with a Forest Service patch on the left sleeve. Green chino pants, still neatly creased after being packed away in anticipation of this day. A brown leather belt. Boots she'd even bothered to clean the night before, by lantern light when it became too dark to read.

A simple uniform, not that different from her standard shirt and jeans, but it meant a lot. Her return to the outside, for one. For most people, the routine she would be entering, of patrolling trails and educating visitors, would be an isolated life, but compared to the quiet of the fire tower, the human contact was overwhelming. The uniform formed a barrier to keep the human world at bay until she was ready for it.

Even David, she admitted. Her skin felt feverish anticipating his touch and the delicate fabric of her panties was already soaked through, but for the first half-hour or so, trying to remember the give and take of conversation was nervewracking. The uniforms, hers and his, helped with that, gave a little formality to the exchange until, by some unspoken signal, they'd know the time for formality was passed.

Was that the Jeep? He had to leave it almost a mile from the tower, but in the quiet, the engine noise carried.

Only one way to be sure.

She couldn't remember the last time she'd made the hike to the access road so quickly. Probably the last time she'd been waiting for David to arrive.

'Long time no see.' Did her voice always sound that hesitant or was it just rusty?

Fortunately, David didn't mind, if his smile were any indication. 'It has been. Too long. It's good to see you.'

She drank him in. Not actually the first human she'd seen since she'd relieved him on fire tower duty, but the first one who mattered as something other than a terse line in her log book. (*July 6: party of three hikers. July 14: two hikers, German; directed them towards Squaw Lake.*) He too was turned out in full kit, although he wore shorts of the same green as her slacks, and he was a bit rumpled from the drive.

She didn't realise she was reaching out her hands until he took them.

Just hands, but the skin contact was enough to make her catch her breath.

In a movie, David would have pulled her into a passionate kiss. Instead, they held position, in contact but at arm's length, just looking at each other. And for the moment, this, her first skin-to-skin contact in ages, was enough to make both her heart and her clit pound.

David was the first to speak. 'Let's head up. The sooner we do . . .' He grinned and blushed a little under his tan.

She grinned back. 'Give me some stuff to carry.'

The short scramble to the cabin and tower seemed to take forever and not just because they were carrying heavy packs and a canvas bag of groceries each. They were both used to that. The trail was too narrow to walk side by side and hold hands, so Karen led the way. She could feel his eyes on her the whole way up.

It was part of the ritual to put away the first load of David's stuff, chatting a bit to let Karen rediscover her voice and David re-accustom to the quiet. 'Looks like you brought less than usual,' she commented.

'No point in more than I'll need for this rotation; we'd just have to carry it out again.'

The can of tomatoes she'd been holding slipped from her fingers. Fortunately, she'd been about to set it on the shelf, so it sounded only like she'd put it down a little hard. 'Don't remind me.'

An awkward silence. Then, to fill it, she said, 'Do you know what you're going to do?'

'I put in for a transfer to Alaska.' His voice dropped at the end of the sentence, as if he expected a bad reaction. 'You?'

They never talked about their outside lives; it was strange to hear it now. Stranger still to articulate.

'I bought some undeveloped land near Eureka years ago,' she said. 'I've been socking money away, clearing the land when I have time to get out there.'

'Sounds like you planned for the inevitable.'

She shrugged. 'I didn't expect them to decommission so many towers so quickly. I was just planning for retirement.'

She didn't want to talk about it any more. Didn't want to think about this being their last meeting. She swallowed past the lump in her throat, took the sack of flour out of his hand, and led him across the room.

The bed was sturdy, but only big enough for one. Years ago, one of them – she'd forgotten which one – had hauled up a queen-sized futon mattress. Normally it stayed folded up in the back of the wardrobe.

In preparation for David's arrival, she'd swept the faded rugs on the floor and laid the futon on top of them, spreading crisp, powder-blue cotton sheets and plumping up the feather pillows. A quilt was folded on the bed, easily reachable to drag over their tired, sated bodies. She'd arranged a grouping of three fat white candles, dried leaves pressed into their waxy surface. They wouldn't light the candles – far too dangerous during the dry season they were here to monitor – but she liked the homey look of them.

David turned to her, took her face in his hands. 'You are a sight for sore eyes,' he said, his tone bordering on wonderment.

Karen's throat tightened. They were both thinking the same thing: that this was their last time. Somehow, the stars had aligned so they'd met here, clicked into a strange, twice-a-year relationship that suited them both.

She wasn't sure if she loved him, because she wasn't sure what love felt like. But she thought that if it did feel anything like this, it must be pretty damn good. She didn't kid herself that this could be more like normal love, like a normal relationship. They both knew they were too set in their ways, too much loners to survive together for any length of time before they turned into snarling, territorial creatures.

She skimmed her thumb over his lower lip, dipping into the cleft in his chin and feeling the prickle where he'd missed a spot shaving.

Accepting the truth didn't make it feel any less bittersweet.

They kissed, his tongue searching for hers. She met him gleefully, feeling the touch resonate. Each six-month wait made the first kiss feel new again, yet still with a sense of homecoming.

She unbuttoned the top few buttons of his shirt so she could press her mouth against his collarbone, drinking in the scent of him. No aftershave or cologne, just the smell of healthy male. She nibbled the spot where his neck met his shoulder, and smiled against him when he caught his breath.

'Ah, Karen.' He rained kisses on her face even as he tugged her shirt free from her waistband. Impatient, wanting to feel his hands on her *now*, she helped him, sighing with happiness when the final button came free. He pushed the shirt back over her shoulders and caught sight of the emerald lace camisole.

'A present I get to unwrap for a new surprise

every time,' he said. He spanned her waist with his large hands, slowly skimming upwards until they rested on her ribcage, just beneath her breasts. Normally she wore a pull-over, functional sports bra, not needing strong support because her breasts were small. The benefit of their size was that when she wore something like this (which was, admittedly, only twice a year), they didn't need support at all.

Her nipples stood out against the lace, begging for attention, and he didn't make her wait. He ran his thumbs over the needy peaks, and she rose up on her toes, the sensation starting a wildfire that rippled down between her legs.

He turned her around and pulled her back against him. She could feel his erection press against her ass. Part of her wanted to drop to her knees, unbuckle his belt, and taste the hard length of him. But another part of her wasn't ready for him to stop teasing her.

This was part of the ritual, part of the pleasure. Kneading and pinching her nipples, he brought her to greater heights of excitement. Her clit throbbed as she wriggled back against him, stimulating him until he, too, was on the edge.

And all the while they gazed out at the most beautiful sunset, the sky afire as the sun sank over the wilderness vista they loved.

She was gasping by the time he stopped, her head spinning as her body sizzled. As if by unspoken agreement, as he tore off his shirt and shucked off his shorts, she divested herself of her boots.

He liked to undress her, so she let him undo her buckle, slide the chinos down her legs. His eyes glittered his approval at the boy shorts that skimmed low on her narrow hips, accentuating the curve of her bottom.

The shadows deepened, and she turned on a single lamp before they knelt together on the futon. His cock made a tent of his red cotton boxers. A smear of fluid darkened the material, further evidence of his excitement.

She loved his cock, long and slender, rising from a thatch of crisp blond hair. Loved its taste, its smooth hardness. Her sex spasmed. She wanted him inside of her, filling her.

He pushed the camisole top up and feasted on her nipples, fingers on one, mouth on the other, then alternating, until she was trembling with need. She ached. He drew his finger along the outside of the close-fitting shorts, and she realised she'd soaked them through. She smelled herself before he tasted her on his fingers, eyes locked with hers and promising so much more.

Not to be outdone, she threaded her fingers through his thick chest hair and tugged gently. Such a different feel to her own body. Beneath her hands, muscles flexed. She tickled his nipples, knowing how sensitive they were. His hand moved back between her legs, stroking her over the lace shorts. The sensation was maddening;

not quite hard enough to push her over the edge, not with a layer of cloth between his hand and her aching clit.

She arched her back, striving to press against him, but he followed her move, backing away at the same speed so the pressure remained constant. She moaned her need, unable to articulate, but it didn't matter – he knew what she wanted.

Hooking his fingers into the waistband, he slowly slid the shorts down her legs. The cool air against her crotch did nothing to quench the burning need, and when he tucked his hands beneath her ass and lowered his face to her, his hot breath fanned the flames higher.

'David . . .'

He drew his tongue along her wet, aching flesh, dipping briefly between her lips and then whispering over her clit. She dangled on the edge of the precipice, as sure as if she leaned over the edge of the fire tower.

Her world centred, focused, shrank down to nothing but the sensation of his tongue against her, flicking harder and faster against her clit.

Flashpoint.

Fire flicked up her spine, connecting her brain and her sex. When she screamed, she knew the sound echoed around the tower before bursting free, resounding into the night air.

When she came down from her orgasm, he had such a self-satisfied grin on his face that she had to laugh.

His lips and chin glistened in the lamp light, and she rose up to lick, catlike, at her own juices.

He was bigger than she was, but she had a sleek line of muscles under her skin. When she pushed him down, he went – not that he put up a fight. She tossed his boxers away, straddled him, and sank down on the hard length of him.

They let out simultaneous sighs.

She leaned down to kiss him again, feeling shock waves resonate as their tongues played and she smelled herself again on his face. Then slowly, so slowly, she raised herself up, feeling every inch of him pull and drag at her nether lips.

When she got to the tip, she knew he expected her to sink down again. But she surprised him. She pulled away, and before he could complain (and, indeed, before she could miss being filled by him) she was between his legs, lapping at his cock to catch even more of the slick wetness she'd left behind.

Sweet and sour, with a hint of spice. If she wasn't so horny, she might have given more than a fleeting thought to the Chinese food she hadn't eaten in six months. Instead, she focused only on him, and herself. Sucking him made her even hotter. She felt herself clench, empty, anticipating when he would be inside her again.

She slid her mouth down the length of him, gently sucking. His reddened cock was burning hot, lit from within.

She could masturbate, she could make herself come when she was alone, but there was nothing like the sensation of a hard cock in her mouth. She swirled her tongue around the tip, flicking against the spot she knew drove him wild. Then she encircled him with her mouth again, her lips tight, and moved up and down, up and down, her hand following the same path.

His hands fisted in the sheets and she knew he was close.

As tempting as it was to make him come in her mouth, she wanted his first orgasm to be inside of her. She gave his cock one final, hard suck, and climbed on top of his stretched naked form, admiring the play of muscles in his chest as he reached up to help guide her down onto him.

Filled again. She paused, her lips against the base of his cock, savouring the moment. But his hands urged her on, as did the bucking of his hips. She leaned back, and he reached up to fondle her nipples. The combined sensation brought her close, so close to the edge.

His breathing quickened, and she knew he was close, too. She urged him on, half demanding and half begging. He thrust up, hard, and behind her eyes the world exploded into fire. She cried out again, grinding herself against him to prolong both her orgasm and his.

At last she fell forwards, sweaty and spent. He

stroked her hair as she nuzzled her head into the hollow of his shoulder.

'Welcome back,' she said.

They roused themselves long enough to have a simple, hearty meal: thick pea soup with chunks of ham heated over the hotplate, accompanied by fresh, crusty French bread he'd brought with him. To finish, they had the final two pieces in a box of Godiva chocolates she'd brought with her six months ago, letting the fine chocolate melt on their tongues and, ultimately, each other.

Karen awoke with the sense that something was wrong. At first she thought it was the unusualness of having a warm body beside her, of someone's deep, regular breathing filling the cabin.

But even after she accepted that, she still felt the unease.

Every time she started a six-month shift at the tower, it took her about a week to get acclimatised, and she had to set an alarm. Now she automatically woke every four hours.

They were spooned together, and she felt his cock twitch and begin to harden against her tailbone. But he didn't protest when she slid away; his sense of responsibility was as strong as hers, and he knew she had a job to do.

He even crawled off the futon and, naked, joined her on the watch with an extra pair of binoculars.

Four a.m. Not as silent as most people supposed. Already the first birds sleepily trilled a greeting to the coming dawn.

The Forestry Commission was already employing satellites to scan the area, ramping up the use of those while they scaled down the searches from various towers. David might be checking only every six hours on his last watch.

She slipped on the night-vision goggles, designed to catch heat sources. She'd do a naked visual scan, too.

Because of her unease, she scanned even more carefully than usual, checking near campsites where she knew people were staying.

So many towers were being decommissioned, all over the country. It was the end of an era. The loss tugged at her, and she wondered if that accounted for her disquiet. It was her last night here. Her last shift ever. Her last time with David, as far as she knew.

She'd never been good with change.

They both spotted it at once. She wasn't prone to flights of fancy, but Karen had the strangest sensation, like a flash of vertigo, that it had taken both of them together to be aware of it.

She recognised the area. There had been campers there recently, but they'd left early yesterday. They obviously hadn't made sure their campfire was completely out.

There was no smoke, not yet. The fire was in

an area of deep underbrush, which meant it smouldered and crept along the ground below the sightline before it broke free above.

A slow burn.

The next hours were a flurry of activity.

Pulling down the alidade, a ceiling-mounted survey instrument, so she could peer through the scope and take a reading to determine where exactly the fire was.

Urgent calls on the radio.

Too-fast drives down bumpy, pitted dirt logging roads to roust out any campers who might be in danger. Further confirmations of the location of the fire.

The *whop-whop-whop* of chopper blades as the fire helicopter scooped up water from Blue Heron Lake and dropped it on the flames.

Then, just as suddenly, it was over. The natural sounds of the forest took over, although in hushed tones, as if the wildlife were counting their blessings. Karen was exhausted, sweaty, and stinking of smoke. David suggested she stay – shower, maybe catch a catnap. The offer of sex was unspoken.

It was oh, so tempting, all of it. To spend more time in her beloved tower, to spend more time with David.

But in the end, she knew it was best to leave on the high note. They'd done their job, the one they came here for. It was a fitting farewell. The climax was over; a denouement would only drag out the inevitable.

She didn't even let him walk her to her Jeep.

She looked back, once, when she got to the vehicle. The tall tower was dark against the bright sky. David's form was silhouetted along the rail.

She took a mental snapshot, and drove away.

Karen's face split into a grin at the expression on David's face when he saw her. He wouldn't have been watching for her arrival, but even so, she'd parked her Jeep half a mile down the road and hiked to sit on the hood of his.

'What – what are you doing here?' he managed.

She laughed and jumped off the hood. 'What, not even a "hello, nice to see you"?'

She barely had time to finish the question before he dropped his pack, gathered her up, and kissed her, swinging her around and around.

When she could catch her breath again, she said, 'Now, *that's* a better greeting.'

'I didn't expect you to be here,' he said.

She jerked her thumb at the tower in the distance. 'I've got a job to do.' She took pity on his befuddlement and continued. 'After we spotted the slow burn six months ago – which neither satellite nor air survey had seen, and wouldn't have until it was much worse – they decided to keep the tower in commission. They reviewed the letters we both had on file arguing against the decommissioning. I even had to speak at the hearing.

'We've been granted our reprieve, David. The tower is still ours.'

They didn't bother unloading the supplies. They each grabbed a backpack and headed for the tower. The narrow trail seemed endless, and when it finally opened out onto the meadow beneath the tower, David took her arm and spun her around, claiming her mouth again.

They never even made it inside.

Fevered hands stripped off clothes, eager to caress the warm flesh beneath. Hot mouths meeting. Flames igniting. He thrust into her, and she gave an exultant cry.

Later, they lay on the prickly browned grass, sweat drying on their skin. A curious bee buzzed close, and she lazily swatted it away.

'I missed you,' David said simply.

And it was enough.

Sophie Mouette is the author of the Black Lace novel, *Cat Scratcher Fever*, and her short fiction has been published in numerous Wicked Words collections. Part of the writing team that is Sophie Mouette also writes as Sarah Dale, whose first novel, *A Little Night Music*, will be published by Cheek in June 2007.

Sweet Charity Monica Belle

'What am I supposed to do, Mrs Townshend?'

'Pick a costume and one of the blue buckets, Lizi, then get out there and get the money in!'

I couldn't help but smile in return for her big cheesy grin, but mainly I felt silly. Charity is charity, but wandering around a shopping centre on a Saturday afternoon dressed in an animal costume? Still, like Neil said, it was for a good cause. I would just have preferred it if Neil had turned up on time.

'Where do we change?'

'In there where the costumes are, dear. Don't be long, most of the team are already out there doing their thing!'

Another cheesy grin and another nervous smile in response. I went into the room she'd showed, which seemed to be some sort of janitor's closet, only there was a pile of bright-blue buckets with the charity logo on the side and a rack of costumes. There were four costumes.

A gorilla. Not really me.

A tortoise. Definitely not me.

A hippo. No way!

A leopard.

That was more like it, slinky with spots, and just about my size. Also furry, and sure to be hot. I hesitated a moment because I had no way of locking the door and anybody might have walked in, before quickly stripping to my knickers. Only then did I discover how difficult it was to get into the leopard suit. There was a zip starting under the tail, so I more or less had to insert myself up the thing's bum, only once I'd got my top half in my legs wouldn't go, leaving me jumping around the room with my knickers on show, which was the exact moment a man I'd never seen before in my life walked into the room.

He smiled, to which I managed to return a sort of leopardy look. I was earnestly wishing I'd kept my bra on, but there was really no choice. I could either stand there looking a complete fool until he'd put his own costume on, and he'd already selected the tortoise, or I could strip off again and hope he was enough of a gentleman not to take a peek at my tits.

'Would you mind turning your back for a second, please?'

'Yeah, sure.'

He turned his back. I removed the leopard suit. He pretended to fiddle with the fittings on the tortoise costume while I climbed back into the leopard suit. I put one leg in, then the second, tugged the material gratefully up over my bum, and discovered that there was no way on Earth I

could get the upper part of my body into it too.
He continued to fiddle with his costume. I wriggled, I writhed, and every single movement
seemed to accentuate my bare breasts.

Finally he spoke up.

'Are you sure you wouldn't like a hand with
that?'

'No ... really, I'm fine.'

'I think you're supposed to take the head off
first.'

He'd half turned, catching himself an eyeful
and a scowl, but he was right. I did have to take
the head off. That way I could undo the zip all
the way and get my arms in, then put the head
back on. The relief as I closed the zip across my
chest was huge, but it was nothing to covering
my face, which must have been roughly the
colour of blackberry juice.

I was dressed, and did my best to maintain a
dignified efficiency as I picked up the bucket and
left the little room. It wasn't that easy, not when
the leopard suit fitted like a second skin, while it
was impossible to walk without the tail bouncing up and down on my bum. Mrs Townshend
gave me her big cheesy grin.

'Go get 'em, girl!'

All she got back was my leopardy look, now
the full range of my expression. I set off with my
tail bouncing behind me, smack into Neil coming
the other way. He recognised me straight off,
probably because he could see every contour I

have through my fur. He kissed my leopardy
nose and gave me a smack on my leopardy bum
before moving on in with just one word.

'Later.'

I knew what he meant, just what he meant,
my favourite little treat for helping him out with
his fundraiser, which you can bet put a spring in
my step. Soon I'd reached the populated area,
and began shaking my bucket, while wishing I'd
had the sense to put some money in it so that it
jingled. I was going to go for the door out to the
car park, but there was this nasty big tiger there
who growled at me, and that wasn't the only
animal in the centre.

A lion and a rhino had staked their pitch on
either side of the main doors, while a pair of
elephants were guarding the lift. A zebra and a
warthog had the mezzanine floor, and there was
a crocodile lurking outside Smith's. I grabbed the
upper mezzanine, shaking my bucket and shaking my tail around the café tables, until I'd got
enough coins to make a decent jingle.

Time for a drink. Off with my leopard head
and I bagged a caramel macchiato to sip while I
looked down on the floor below. Now we had
the whole menagerie out, and the last three
animals had taken the main aisle on the first
floor. My peeping tortoise had the lift station,
right underneath me. I could have poured coffee
right down the back of his shell, only it wouldn't
have been fair. He had tried to be a gentleman.

Some goofball had gone for the hippo suit, and he was making a serious fool of himself, dancing about with his monstrous backside wobbling behind, and I say 'his' because it had to be a man. No woman could ever bring herself to behave like such a complete idiot. I had to laugh.

Then there was the gorilla, my gorilla. It had to be Neil, as there was no way he was the hippo. I rather liked him as a gorilla. No, I fancied him as a gorilla. Maybe it was my accidental bit of exposure, maybe it was his naughty promise, maybe I was just in a horny mood, but it was kind of fun and kind of kinky. Maybe when I'd got a bit more money I'd start to stalk him, and pounce on him. Then we'd see what happened.

I went back to work, or rather, hunting, stalking the tables, pouncing on lone individuals who stopped for a drink, picking off the stragglers in the café queue. When a female stopped to get her brood chocolates I was right there behind her, helping them keep their weight down and saving them from the dentist. When a huge old bull paused to count his change I was lingering hopefully beside him. When I spotted a fine young male coming up in the lift I was ready to get him.

Before too long my bucket was getting heavy. I was beginning to feel I'd done my share and maybe it was time to think about my main prey. A glance from the balcony showed he was still about, as big and black and hairy as ever, scratching his armpits in the hope of extracting change from a herd of little old ladies. He hadn't seen me and I moved back from the edge, now stalking in earnest.

The lift was glass, too open. I sneaked down a flight of stairs and on out onto the first floor, keeping to the cover of a stand of umbrellas. He was as before, unsuspecting as he fed a pastrami on ciabatta into his gaping maw. Now was my moment, to take him while he was eating. I crept closer, from stand to stand, stall to stall, answering the cheeky comment of a cockney costermonger with a hiss and a swish of my tail, my attention fully on my prey.

Still eating, the hapless gorilla had begun to walk away from me, towards the tinkling fountain at the centre of the first-floor plaza – a fatal mistake. I crept closer on velvet paws, any sound I might have made muffled by the water, my every sense alert, one leg in front of the other, slowly, softly, and a final rush, to allow my hand to close on one firm masculine buttock within the hairy confines of his gorilla suit.

He nearly left the planet, dropping the piece of sandwich he had in his hand and choking on the piece he hadn't. Two pats on the back, a little purr and a little rub and I'd fled, treating him to an insolent wiggle of my tail as he stood gaping, more like a goldfish than a gorilla. I'd thought he would chase me, and planned a careful line of retreat so that if he did catch me there would be nobody to see what I got for my cheek.

I didn't get anything, not even a little run to get me breathless and wanting it. He just stayed where he was. It was typical Neil, all horny for me in the bedroom but too shy to be a little daring. I knew what to do about that. First things first though, my social responsibilities as a leopard in aid of famine, and then I could deal with my own rather different hunger.

Mrs Townshend oohed and aahed over my contribution and said several things with exclamation marks. I gave her my best leopardy look, emptied my bucket and went back to the fray. She was right. I'd done well, and now it was time for a little fun. I was going gorilla hunting, in earnest.

First, I needed a lair. Mrs Townshend had one, so maybe there was one above it? A brief foray confirmed that there was, and better still, unused. Next, there was that special little something, my naughty secret. A brief attack on a pair of penguins escorting some young and I'd collected enough in my bucket to fulfil my needs. Now I really was a naughty girl, using charity money for improper purposes, highly improper purposes. I would give it back, of course, but it was still naughty, and I like that.

I knew my territory now, and made Abigail's Accessories without the gorilla spotting me.

Abigail, or possibly one of her assistants, supplied me with what I needed, a dinner candle of the short variety, just right for naughty girls, or even a naughty leopard girl. I was glad she couldn't see my face, because you know that when a single girl buys a single candle it's not necessarily going in a stick.

Now for the hunt. I had my tummy fluttering, and felt as naughty as naughty can be. Out on the mezzanine the zebra had stopped to browse and the warthog was snuffling around a likely looking troop of housewives. I slunk past, taking care not to be seen from above, and as I climbed the stairs I saw my prey. He was at the far end of the aisle, holding his bucket out to a pair of suits, his shaggy black back towards me.

I crept forwards in the shelter of the stalls, ignoring a yet cheekier comment from my cockney costermonger and sidling sideways into the shadow of a stand of sunglasses. Still the gorilla talked. I moved forwards, loath to interrupt his foraging but determined I would get him this time. Slowly I crept forwards, from shadow to shadow, from Woolies to Marks to Macs, the last ensuring that he had no chance of picking up my scent on the wind.

At last the suits moved on. I stepped out boldly, walking up beside him to run a hand down his furry back to his furry buttocks. He jumped just like before, but I'd already moved away, this time taunting with a deliberate wiggle of my leopardy tail and an ever so meaningful crook of one leopardy finger. Now he came after me, slow and steady, six foot six of hairy black gorilla with his eyes fixed on my wiggling tail. I sped up. He sped up too, and we were running laughing down the aisle, oblivious to everyone's the stares.

Where I wanted to go there was nobody to stare, just the blank end of the side passage and the door to some offices, unoccupied on a Saturday. My own little nook was open, and I slid inside, my head poked out, one finger to beckon and one long leopardy leg to entice. He came on, now eager, hunched low and scratching under one arm, then stood high to beat his chest and show off what a big strong dominant male he was. I already knew.

I slipped inside. He followed. I jammed the door with a chair and cuddled close, rubbing my body against him to feel the power of him against my breasts and tummy and legs. I nuzzled his face as he returned my embrace, his hands slipping low to cup my bottom, so like a man, impatient, but now I didn't care. I let him feel, his big hairy gorilla hands cupping my furry cheeks, squeezing and feeling with all the ardour of the first ever time, for all that he'd held me a hundred. He only let go when he lifted his hands to his head, but I shook mine.

'Uh-uh, I want you the way you are. Be a gorilla for me, only I want my special treat too.'

He answered with a grunt, just right. I ducked down to my bucket, feeling the heat in my cheeks as I took out the candle. He knew, he'd seen, he'd done it for me a dozen times, but it still made me blush, so hot, and that heat went straight where it belonged, hotter still as I whispered into his ear.

'You know where this goes, don't you?'

This time I got a double grunt. He took the candle. I was purring as I went down, eager to be taken straight away, and as I was. There were lots of chairs, just right for a naughty girl to kneel on while she gets her special treat. I chose one and climbed right on, pushing out my furry bottom and reaching back to lift my tail, surely all the invitation any man could ever need?

It was all he needed. He gave a single throaty grunt and closed in. I gave him a wiggle and closed my eyes, eager to lose myself in my fantasy as he gave me what I so badly needed. I felt his hands on my body, tracing the outline of my hips and thighs, my bottom and my breasts, stroking me through my fur. His front pressed to me and already I could feel the big excited bulge beneath his suit, ready for my body, ready to fill me right up to the top of my head.

I gave him another wiggle, encouraging him, and his hands had found my zip. My mouth came open in a sigh as he drew it down, nice and slow, allowing my costume to open and make me available to his big gorilla hands, his big gorilla mouth, his big gorilla cock. Now I hung my head, leaning on the chair, my back pulled in and my knees set wide, presenting myself to him the way he likes me, the way he knows means he can do as he pleases, especially that one special thing.

He began to touch, the hair on his hands tickling my cheeks and between, to make my muscles tighten in anticipation. I sighed again as he ducked down low, nuzzling his face in between my cheeks to rub my pussy and send shiver after shiver of pure joy all the way up my spine to my head. He had my costume right open, my bottom pushing out of the unzipped hole, bare and wide, everything showing in an open invitation for what I wanted. I heard the rustle of the crinkly plastic of the candle wrapping and I could hold back my words no more.

'Put it in ... go on, right in ... nice and slow.'

I spread my knees wider still as I spoke, really flaunting myself, like the naughty rude little show-off I am. He could see the target, I knew, my back pulled in as far as it could go, my cheeks spread wide, open and ready, ready for the candle to be slid in where it belonged, right up my pussy, slid in to give me just a teasing touch of that gorgeous full feeling and drawn slowly in and out, fucking me, tormenting me. I let him do it, knowing he was only getting me ready for the real thing and that the more he teased the better it would be when I got it. In and out went the candle, making me gasp and sigh, wriggle my bum and clutch at the chair, until at last I couldn't bare it any more.

'Go on, you bastard, do it ... do it, will you? Make me ready and just ... just fucking do it!'

I screamed out the last words, but all he did was move the candle in and out, faster still, until I was whimpering with frustration and need. He was doing it on purpose, I knew, because he wanted me to say it, like the dirty little schoolboy he was at heart, like most men are. Not that I could resist, and he knew it, but I was wiggling my toes and thumping my hand on the back of the chair in frustration before I finally cracked and the dirty words began to spill from my lips.

'Up my bum, you bastard! That's what you want to hear, isn't it? Now do it ... stick it up my bum ... stick it ...'

My words broke to a long low sigh as he obliged. I felt the candle touch me in that so naughty place. I felt myself open, accepting the long hard shaft deep inside me. It felt so nice, holding me just a little open and filling me up, but better, far better, it felt so naughty, so gloriously naughty, to have something up my bottom and in front of a man.

I was whimpering with pleasure as he let go of the candle shaft, leaving it deep inside me with just a little bit sticking out, and purring as I positioned myself for entry and gave him one more encouraging wiggle. It's so nice to feel bare and to feel rude in front of a man, a man who appreciates my feelings and responds to me, a man like Neil. He knows what I'm like too, and what I'd be thinking as I knelt for him, open and ready behind, with a candle up my bum, as he quickly adjusted his suit to pull himself free. Now it was gorilla time.

He gave a throaty grunt as he moved up behind me, making me giggle even as I felt the hot hard head of his cock press to my leg. One huge hairy hand moved down between my thighs and he was guiding himself into me, bringing my mouth wide in a gasp of pure bliss as I felt myself open and fill. I adore that full feeling. There is nothing like it in all this world, and now I had it, in my own special way and more, kneeling, with something up my bum and a gorgeous great gorilla to fuck me.

In he went, all the way, until I could feel the thick shaggy fur against my bottom, ticklish and warm. His hands found my hips, holding me tight as he began to move inside me, back and forth, in and out, and with every push jamming the candle in to remind me that it was up my bottom. I was gasping immediately, wriggling myself onto him and drumming my feet on the chair for the sheer overwhelming ecstasy of what he was doing to me.

He felt bigger than ever, although I was accepting him with ease. It was as if he was filling not just my pussy but the whole of my being, right up to the top of my head, which is exactly the way it should be. He was good too, taking his time, slow and deep, then hard and fast, and slow and deep once more, until I was dizzy with pleasure and knew that all I needed was that one tiny crucial touch to take me over the edge.

I tried to hold off, savouring the pleasure he was giving me, but it was just too much. My hand went back, but as I found my sex he grunted. My own hand was gently but firmly removed from between my thighs, only to be replaced with his own, or rather his big hairy gorilla paw. It was something he'd never done before, one more rude, loving detail to our repertoire, and I was babbling thanks even as he began to rub me.

He was fucking me too, short awkward thrusts, as he held onto me around my belly and hip, but hard and satisfying, while his body was pressed tight against my bum to make the candle move with each and every push. I was going to come, my vision hazy with pleasure as I let my hand stray to my chest, stroking my painfully stiff nipples through my fur as my feelings rose, with my entire mind concentrated on what he was doing to me, how well he had handled me.

As my thighs and tummy went tight a moan escaped my lips. I thought of how I'd teased him, wiggling my spotted furry bottom until he decided to have me despite the risk of where we were. I thought of how I'd bent over for him, my bum pushed out first in fur and then bare naked for his attention. I thought of how he'd teased me, easing the candle in and out of my pussy when he knew full well where it was supposed to go, until I'd broken and begged for it. I thought of how he'd fucked me, how he was still fucking me, how we'd look, me with my bare bottom sticking out of my leopard suit while I was humped by a big hairy gorilla. I thought of what he was doing, bringing me off under his fingers as he fucked me, and with that I came.

I screamed and I screamed again, oblivious to the danger of getting caught, and I would have screamed some more if one great hairy hand hadn't closed over my mouth. He held me like that, still fucking me, still rubbing me, tight in his grip as I rode my orgasm, through one blinding peak after another, until at last I could hold on to it no more.

With that he took his own pleasure, gripping me by the hips and driving himself deep so hard he had me gasping again immediately. I was so sensitive I thought my head would burst as I shook it urgently from side to side, but he was done almost immediately, whipping his cock free at the very last instant to speckle my bum with hot wet seed.

I had barely come down from my high when we heard the sound of voices, and there was a frantic scrabble to get ourselves decent. Whoever it was passed by, but with my excitement gone so had my daring, and we left our cubbyhole as quickly as we could, sneaking out one by one to mingle with the shopping crowds once more, only now I was wearing a happy grin under my leopard mask as I worked.

Twice more that afternoon I passed the gorilla as we came and went with our buckets, and each time I gave him a little squeeze where it would do the most good. I was keen to get home too, feeling a little sticky and up for more fun, so I went down to Mrs Townshend as soon as I decently could. She didn't mind, happy with my takings, and I quickly changed back, no longer a leopard girl.

I was just doing up my second shoe when I heard Neil's voice behind me.

'How did it go, Lizi? Did you enjoy it?'

He knew full well I had and I turned to give him a cheeky answer, to find myself looking up at a large hippo.

Monica Belle is the author of the Black Lace novels *Noble Vices*, *Valentina's Rules*, *Wild in the Country*, *Wild by Nature*, *Office Perks*, *Pagan Heat* and *The Boss*. Her stories have also appeared in several Wicked Words collections.

Missionary Impossible
Maya Hess

Nadia Kasparova read the brief. Her eyes moved slowly, incredulously, across the screen as if they were revolving freely in their sockets, as weightless and relaxed as her dangling limbs. She pulled down the hem of her T-shirt, tucking it into the waistband of her sweatpants, and closed her eyes. Wiping away droplets of sweat that had beaded on her recently exercised body, Nadia recalled her years of training. She fast-forwarded everything that she had worked for, replaying it through her mind in order to focus on the latest and highly unusual set of experiments to be carried out on the World Space Station *Ventura*.

'Two hundred and eighty-three days and it has not entered my mind.' Nadia opened her eyes and exhaled heavily. Later, she would be drinking her breath in the form of recycled air. Water was precious three hundred miles above the Earth. 'Up here, I feel barely human. Why do they think I would want to act like one?' She read the brief again, just to make sure: 'Operation EROSS –

Experimental Reproduction in Orbiting Space Station ... preparation for sexual reproduction during long-term space missions by husband–wife teams ... possible approaches to sexual relations in the zero-G environment ...'

Nadia switched screens to monitor her other experiments and smiled. She felt comfortable with the tables and graphs that presented strings of numerical information relating to her beloved seedlings. Studying the effect of microgravity on fast-growing plants was the first step to becoming self-sufficient in space during manned missions to Mars and beyond. Not only would the specimens eventually provide a supply of food, but they would also assist with reconditioning waste water and stale air.

How could they possibly expect her to divert her attention to *this* ridiculous new experiment?

'Pfah! I will not do it. My contract states my work and this –' Nadia flicked the monitor with her clipped fingernails '– this is what I am paid to do.' She left the cramped work space and retreated weightlessly to her tiny cabin, making use of the anchor points along the way. She began to mutter in Russian while she unfastened her comfort pack and withdrew a limited number of wet wipes. Unable to rid her usually clear and focused mind of the new brief from Mission Control, Nadia stripped naked and began to vigorously rub the sweat from her body before it could bead and escape into the cabin. She used tooth powder and dry shampoo and applied a smear of moisturiser – her only luxury – before dressing in that week's allocated clean clothing.

'Brig, I'm turning in. Is everything OK your end?' Nadia used the intercom to speak to Commander Robert Brigson.

'I'm just sending reports downstairs for tomorrow's docking procedures. Things are looking good for a clean swap and, boy, I can't wait for something different to eat.'

Nadia smiled, although wouldn't have done if she was speaking with the commander face to face. Robert was easy to get along with, as professional as they came yet strangely casual about falling around the Earth at eighteen thousand miles per hour. By 'downstairs', he meant Mission Control in Florida.

'And we'll have a new friend.' Nadia cleared her throat of whatever was caught there – perhaps the thought of a new crew member sent specifically to assist with the radical experiments, or perhaps just the tooth powder. You couldn't spit in space. Swallowing was imperative.

'Drew? You'll love him. We were in the Air Force together in the nineties. Nadia, take a look out of your window.'

The intercom went silent for a moment as Nadia turned to the blackness outside. A small but brilliant spangle fizzed over Asia and within seconds had reared up over the planet, spreading its dazzling fingers around the edge of the Earth, making it look like a giant diamond solitaire ring. But only for a few moments, and then the invasive rays of the sun drenched the interior of the space station in annoying heat and light.

'That was nice. I'm tired. Good night, Brig.' Nadia strapped herself into the sleeping bag, which in turn was strapped to a bulkhead, and snapped a mask over her eyes to seal out the light. She sighed. In eighteen hours, the delivery spacecraft *Evolution* would deposit Mission Specialist Captain Drew Masters along with supplies of food, clean clothing and equipment for the laboratory. She struggled to get comfortable as the sunlight filtered through her mask. 'Damned sunrise happens every ninety minutes anyway.' Nadia squirmed onto her side and slipped angrily into her allotted eight hours of sleep. Her fitful dreams were filled with feeble excuses why she wouldn't conduct the ridiculous experiments and the new crew member forcing himself upon her in the name of science. Finally, she slept.

Nadia was woken by piped classical music, courtesy of Mission Control.

'Good morning, Miss Kasparova. Another beautiful day.'

Nadia recognised the voice as Brigitte's, assistant controller in Florida. It was comforting to know that every breath she inhaled, every experiment she undertook and every piece of food she ate was monitored and logged by scores of trained professionals back on Earth. Nadia was convinced that they could read her thoughts too – and she wouldn't have minded, either. Her brain was so honed and sharpened for life in space that there was nothing she wouldn't share with any of the staff back at base. Being an astronaut wasn't simply a job: it was her life.

'Hello, Brigitte. You have sunshine today?' Nadia pushed the mask up into her glossy blonde hair, cropped into a boyish style, and peeled apart the webbing that had held her in place. There was a lag before Brigitte's crackled reply beeped into the cabin.

'Still eighty-four degrees and the sun's going down. Now listen, Nadia, we've been working with your commander for the last few hours but he's resting now in readiness for the docking. All is on schedule and in T minus nine hours forty minutes you're going to have yourself a new buddy.' More static.

Nadia swallowed, remembering yesterday's unexpected brief. 'Buddy?'

Brigitte came back. 'Yeah, you know, like friend, pal ... er, mate?'

'I know what buddy means.' Nadia was sensitive about her English, aware that her accent tolled with the harsh, almost manly, tones of her native Russian. She was jolted by a sudden wave of terror – something she hadn't experienced since her last solo space walk. 'Mate?' She knew the word meant friend as well as sexual partner, neither of which she wanted.

'You'll love him. And besides, you've got chocolate and gum coming. It's your lucky day, Miss Kasparova.'

Usually, Nadia enjoyed Brigitte's jovial company. Men made up the majority of the team in Florida, so conversing with Brigitte fulfilled a small requirement in her psyche for female company. She was precise and strict about satisfying basic requisites during a mission but resisted the more obvious and urgent human desires. Nadia considered herself as polished and intricate as the equipment that maintained their orbit. She was a faultless machine.

'I don't eat candy and I don't need company when I'm working.' Nadia retrieved her trainers from a locker and put on her crew zip-up jacket, every languorous movement a fight against freedom, a struggle against the precision of Nadia's mind. Her body wanted to drift aimlessly around the cabin while her brain was eager to get to work.

Brigitte briefed Nadia on various routine duties before tentatively mentioning Operation EROSS. 'It really is your lucky day, then, don't you think?'

Nadia recognised the overzealous banter for what it was. In her head, she thought in Russian but, when she spoke, her words were clipped and brisk English.

'My contract does not state that I must copulate with fellow crew members. I object strongly to the nature of this experiment.' Nadia waited impatiently beside the communication panel. She wanted to get to the lab.

'I don't think you're expected to copulate, Nadia. It's merely a simulation and apparatus evaluation for future missions. In years to come, as the space station grows and develops, married couples will live up there for months at a time. We can hardly expect them to, well, abstain.' More static interfered with the transmission. Nadia sighed, preventing herself from floating upside down in relation to the panel by gripping a strap. 'Nadia, are you still there?'

As mission specialist in charge of the laboratory, Nadia knew she would have to comply with orders. As she mentally scanned the fine print of her contract, she realised that several clauses bound her to fulfil her duties unless severe psychological deficiencies made such work impossible. For Nadia, the admission that she was not mentally fit for her work was worse than having to test the sexual apparatus with the newcomer.

'I'm still here.' She paused again, suddenly aware of the language and culture barrier as she attempted to put her feelings into words. 'I would have preferred to know this several weeks ago, so that I can prepare myself for this sexual activity.'

'Nadia, *no*, repeat, *no*.' The stern voice of the chief mission controller suddenly resounded through the beeps and static. 'Your orders do not include sexual intercourse. Repeat, do not have sexual intercourse aboard *Ventura*.'

'Yes, sir,' Nadia replied, dazed by the notion that anyone would consider her capable of such an activity. She couldn't recall the chief ever being so fervent, except when she successfully fixed one of the solar panels that hung like giant wasp wings from *Ventura*'s cylindrical body. 'Kasparova out.'

She left the cabin and steered her weightless, unusually irrepressible body to the laboratory. For the first time ever, Nadia wasn't sure that she was entirely in control of her actions. For the first time ever, Nadia's thoughts weren't completely focused on work.

Captain Drew Masters emerged from the transfer compartment of the axial docking port at 04.00 hours Florida time. The *Evolution* spacecraft had executed a flawless deposit of food supplies, clothing, technical equipment and one or two personal supplies, the last of which Nadia had not requested. Comfort, she believed, was for life on Earth.

'Welcome.' Commander Brigson assisted Masters as he emerged through the hatch. The two men attempted a brief embrace but settled for a handshake when their bodies refused to combine in the weightless surroundings. Nadia smiled. She didn't expect Operation EROSS to get much further than their clumsy attempts at bodily contact.

'Captain Masters.' Nadia nodded as she was introduced to the American. 'I hope you will find your time aboard pleasurable and productive.' The two men grinned and exchanged lewd glances.

'I don't envy you, Drew. You have a heavy schedule, I believe.' Commander Brigson studied his associate. 'Although, having read your mission brief last month, I gather that several enjoyable activities will ensue.' Brigson allowed himself a laugh, even though he knew Nadia would disapprove. It was tough working along-side the most perfect human being in the universe.

Nadia gasped. 'You knew?' She forced her hand to connect with her mouth, something that should have taken place with a short, precise movement but lost its impact with a slow-motion attempt at surprise. 'You knew that I would be testing this ... this ... apparatus with a stranger and you didn't warn me?' Eyes as deep as space bored into Commander Brigson. He raised his hands slowly in defence.

'The chief and I thought it best not to tell you too soon. We knew you'd fret. It's a very unusual experiment and highly classified. The world must not know about these investigations.' He paused for a moment, reading the Russian woman's stunning, angular features. He wouldn't have minded a go at trying out the apparatus with her himself, although couldn't imagine what contraptions the scientists back in Florida had come up with. 'It's not like you really have to *do* it, Nadia. You can keep your clothes on.'

'You two do it, then,' she snapped. 'If it's that casual, then be my guest and experiment until your heart is of the content.'

'Heart's content,' Drew Masters chipped in, bemused by Nadia's reluctance. 'We say heart's content where I come from.'

Nadia resisted informing the newcomer that they were nowhere near where he came from so she could use whatever turn of phrase she wished, and, in her usual calm and professional manner, she breathed deeply and took a heart-slowing look at the giant blue ball that six and a half billion people called home. Nadia wasn't sure if she did any more. The sight of it reduced everything to its correct proportions. Within the frame of the porthole was the soup of all life, human or otherwise, bubbling and burning, simmering and steaming, loving and hating, breathing and dying – and reproducing, she thought, every single one of them. Suddenly, she felt godlike, as if she would be serving mankind by conducting the experiments.

A thin line of smile, as much as she could bear

to allow, seeped from Nadia's lips as she realised the implications. 'I'll do it,' Nadia said quietly. 'All in the name of science, you understand, and my continued commitment to *Ventura*.'

The two men nodded and commenced stowing the fresh supplies. Nadia wondered whether they had ever really doubted her dedication, assuming that because she was a woman she would comply with whatever orders were issued. To a certain extent, that was true, but only Nadia herself knew how tough she was and how much she would oppose anything that went against her morals. Trained and sharpened to the limits of human capabilities, Nadia's mind was as tight and lean and finely bound as the muscles that wrapped around her long bones.

Later, Commander Brigson suggested that they eat beef goulash and peas followed by butter-scotch pudding in celebration of the new astro-naut's arrival. Drew watched as Nadia typed the meal request into the computer to locate the correct stowage locker. In the cramped galley, she skilfully manoeuvred herself from the food compartments to the small oven, opening and arranging the foil packets. Drew admired her self-control. He admired, too, the way her mind obviously latched on to every task, whether it be simple food preparation or an intricate exper-iment. Nadia's cool reputation reverberated around Mission Control like an ice-hockey puck.

'I suggest we waste no time in testing the

prototypes. They're keen to get initial results both visually and via written reports.' Drew caught a stray piece of foil as it aimlessly drifted towards the air-filtration duct. He placed it in the trash compactor.

'You mean they're going to watch us?' Nadia kept her eyes on the food, incredulous that not only would she have to entangle herself with a stranger but also that any number of people on Earth would be watching.

'Of course, but you must understand that we're simply checking the viability of certain methods.' Drew turned away before half coughing, half speaking, 'Testing positions.'

'We must make this over with as soon as possible.' Nadia fastened the food containers to trays with Velcro strips and issued their rations.

'*Get* this over with,' Drew corrected but Nadia pretended not to hear.

Commander Brigson was attending to routine maintenance and knew Nadia well enough to allow her privacy while in the laboratory. As Drew grappled and unwrapped various contraptions, Nadia reluctantly set up the communication cameras from five different locations in preparation for the broadcast to Earth. Quick-fire Russian pounded through her head, trying to convince herself that, by performing the sensitive experiments, she would not compromise her professionalism.

'Christ, what are they thinking we should do with this?' Drew laughed and waved it around. The web of grey nylon strapping broke free from his grip and somersaulted through the laboratory. Nadia arrested it and studied it disdainfully.

'It looks like a complicated chastity belt, not something that would make you want to...' Nadia found herself unable to finish.

'You can say "have sex" or "fuck", you know. I won't be shocked and it won't make me think any less of you.'

Nadia's cheeks coloured and, to her horror, she realised the blush was not completely derived from Drew's comment. She turned as quickly as microgravity would allow and zipped up her crew jacket. She wanted to make sure that there was as little of her flesh showing as possible and also the greatest thickness of fabric between them.

'Right, let's get cracking, then.' Drew then made their intentions clear to Mission Control and Nadia made a point of completely ignoring the cameras. She didn't want anyone to see the fear in her eyes.

'Slip your legs in here.' Drew assisted Nadia as she threaded her long, slim legs through what she discovered was an elastic contraption designed to pin the two participants together face to face.

'Of course, this works the other way around, too.' Drew winked at Nadia as he inserted his legs through the holes and pulled the straps tight, locking their groins together in an uncomfortable clinch.

'Ouch!' Nadia pushed on Drew's shoulders. It was bad enough having their legs entangled but for their faces to be at such an intimate distance was intolerable. 'What do you mean, the other way around?' They floated helplessly around the laboratory. All protruding instruments and dangerous objects had been stowed at Drew's request and Nadia had scowled when he implied things could get pretty wild.

'I can take you from behind if I strap myself to your back, if that's what madam would prefer.' Drew grinned but then recoiled in slow motion as Nadia's hand buffeted the side of his head.

'That would have been a sharp slap on Earth. Just get on and do what you have to and then let's get out of this stupid thing.' She turned her face sideways and screwed up her eyes, refusing to wrap her arms around Drew's back as he was doing to her. She couldn't help but notice the citrus tang of real shampoo and the laundry freshness of his clothing, leftovers from regular Earth life and likely to haunt her understimulated nose for days to come.

'What on Earth are you doing?' Nadia felt her body being bumped as they tumbled around the lab.

Drew laughed, risking another slap. 'On Earth,

Miss Kasparova, we call this making love.' He thrust his strapped-up hips even faster, grinding against Nadia's sweatpants, feeling the V-shape and gentle mound at the top of her legs. 'What do you call it?'

Nadia tried to shut down all of her senses, but the breathy words that left Drew's mouth in time to the pulsing delivered by his hips refused to allow such an escape. 'I don't call being strapped to a stranger against my will making love, Captain Masters, on Earth or anywhere else.'

At that moment, Nadia was ashamed of her body. Not for the toned lines and feminine shape it presented to her pseudo-mate but for the way that it responded to the situation. Nadia could barely accept the internal system error that she was diagnosing and was grateful at least that her mind prevented reciprocal thrusts that the surge of warmth in her belly was urging her to try.

Communication from Florida slowed Drew's thrusting hips. Instinctively, he rotated his pelvis in an experienced way – the way a man would hold himself on the brink of orgasm while nursing his lover's nipples or reaching down to trace a figure of eight at the top of her sex.

'How does that feel?' The chief's voice quivered through the miles, distorted by distance and interference.

'Somewhat awkward, and I suspect in practice

this traditional position would be completely impossible,' Drew replied. 'With each forward movement I make to simulate copulation, Nadia's pelvis is shunted away with such a force that even the harness isn't enough to hold her steady. I would float right out of her.'

'Do you feel you are being ... er ... pushed beyond the limits of realistic sexual activity, Miss Kasparova?'

Silence and several beeps as Nadia floated through the laboratory with Drew Masters attached to her groin. She was quite unable to speak.

'I'll take that as an affirmative, Miss Kasparova. Perhaps you could try the harness in reverse. The experts say that a better purchase on the pelvic region can be obtained by securing the female around the upper body with the arms.'

'Copy, chief. Give us a few minutes.' Drew unhitched the harness and Nadia floated away, although she was soon retrieved by a firm grip around her wrist. 'We have work to do. Put this on again but backwards.' Drew leaned in and whispered through Nadia's neat blonde hair. 'Then I have to grip your tits.' He grinned as she recoiled but, unable to escape the impending connection, Nadia sighed and allowed the fullness of her bottom cheeks to be bound against Drew's groin.

'Where's the fifth camera?'

'Below the work station,' Nadia snapped. Her words were followed by a sharp gasp as foreign sensations wound around her body. It took several seconds to realise that Drew's hands were cupping her weightless breasts, his fingers teasing her forgotten nipples into gravity-defying peaks even through the thickness of her jacket. It took several more seconds to realise that Drew had positioned them where his advances would go unnoticed by the cameras.

Nadia mentally kicked herself for the moan that escaped her throat as Drew continued to tease her breasts. If she told him to get off, then Mission Control would know that something was going on and, if she tried to ignore him, well, she wasn't sure how long she could hold back the second gasp that was begging to leave her chest.

'Do you have to do that?' She twisted her head around so she could speak in a whisper, but her mouth was met by Drew's open lips. It was as close to a kiss as Nadia had come in several years.

'Just trying to make the simulation realistic.' Drew grinned and wrapped his legs firmly around the outside of Nadia's thighs so that his now virtually erect cock was nestled in the groove between her fleshy cheeks. Embarrassed by his sudden reaction to Nadia's proximity, he was hoping to conceal his hardness.

'It feels *too* realistic for my liking.' Nadia

wriggled away from the bulge pressed into her bottom but it followed her, growing firmer and more invasive through the soft fabric of her jogging bottoms. 'Can't we try something else? I'm beginning to sweat with this much exertion.'

'You're just not used to it.' Drew growled the words in her ear before pushing his cock into her buttocks as far as he could while tweaking both nipples.

'Exactly what do you mean by that, Captain Masters?' Nadia almost squealed his name as she felt her wretched and faithless body responding.

'That you haven't had it for years, have you, Miss Kasparaova?'

'Get off my back. Now!' Nadia struggled and kicked, and finally Drew unhitched them and they drifted apart. Nadia lifted the hem of her T-shirt, exposing her flat stomach, and wiped her face before the perspiration had a chance to bead and float off her skin. She hated the buzzing inside her jogging bottoms and, so foreign was the sensation, she wondered if a bee had stowed away and found its way into her knickers. She wanted to press her fingers down there to arrest the tingling, but touching herself in front of Drew would be tantamount to admitting she had enjoyed their simulated sex. Nadia forced her mind to overcome her body. These feelings – this *arousal* – simply would not do.

'*Ventura* to Mission Control,' Drew called out. 'Harness proved more promising from rear docking position but unwilling subject made simulation difficult.' Drew grinned at Nadia.

'I am not a piece of space junk. Do you think you can dock me?' She flushed and wiped her face on her T-shirt again, allowing Drew a delicious view of the lower portion of her breasts. He didn't realise that military-issue bras could be so alluring.

'What do you propose is the answer, Captain? The research department are keen for solutions.' The chief's voice rattled through the static.

'Personally, I'd suggest dinner, wine, soft lighting, more wine, a bit of dirty talk, even more wine and then tying her up and giving her one. But, like I said, subject unwilling, so results are unreliable.' Drew laughed and began to pack away the harness. 'Allow me to lavish some of my charm on the subject and we'll see what we can do later. There's still the inflatable tube to try. *Ventura* out.'

Nadia watched as Drew left the laboratory. Was that it? she wondered. She felt empty, somehow cheated. He hadn't even offered a parting kiss. And she was so consumed with thoughts of Drew's body shunting them around the lab that she completely forgot to shut down the audio and visual connection with Mission Control. It wouldn't be until later that she realised her mistake.

* * *

Nadia usually worked right through her daily rest periods. Breaking the flow of concentration, she believed, was detrimental to her productivity. She only allowed herself to eat, wash and sleep outside of the laboratory.

But today, after the unusual encounter with Drew Masters, Nadia retired to her cabin during the next break. She slowly stripped off her clothing as if it were contaminated, knowing that she would have to put it back on at some point because garments had to last several days at least. She allowed her long fingers to brush over her skin, thankful that her body was free from the ridiculous strapping and the incorrigible Masters.

'How do I get out of this mess?' she considered, while floating freely around the small space in just her white bra and knickers. She hugged her body, concerned that these extraordinary circumstances would challenge the strict control she self-inflicted. She stroked her shoulders and, to her utter shock, she allowed her fingers to slip inside the cotton of her bra and cup the fullness of her breasts. Is this how it felt for Drew? she wondered. Intrigued, Nadia trailed a hand down her lower back and nestled it in the fleshy groove between her buttocks. She smiled. It had been a long time.

'I am not completely without feeling,' she whispered in Russian, trying to ignore that her fingers were nuzzling beneath the elastic of her panties in search of the renewed tingle. Nadia bit her bottom lip as she made contact with the awakening bud nestled between the soft folds, following the channel further until she was able to tentatively slip a finger inside her surprisingly moist sex. 'Not at all without feeling,' she told herself, wondering how she would justify this indulgence over tending to fragile seedlings.

'Nadia, you in there?' Drew's voice drove through the bulkhead, causing her to withdraw her hand. Unaccustomed to spending any length of time semi-naked, Nadia forgot her state of undress and concentrated on steering herself to the cabin entrance. Drew's face acted like a mirror as she slid the door open, his shocked but then approving expression reminding Nadia that she was wearing only a bra and knickers.

'Oh! I was just changing. You caught me –'

'No need. You look fine as you are. How about another romp around the lab? We can practise our moves and then show the chief how it's really done. What d'you say?'

Common sense had been shed with her clothing and Nadia wasn't sure if it was the slow, dragging gaze that Drew applied to her naked flesh or the newly discovered sensations that caused her to float out of her cabin and follow him to the lab.

'Brig's sleeping, so there's no one to bother us.'

The laboratory door closed automatically behind the pair as they entered.

'What's that?' She batted away what looked like an inflatable kid's toy bobbing about on a pool.

'That,' said Drew proudly, 'is our reproductive tunnel of love, as supplied by the kind folks in research. Wanna try it out?' His smooth American accent contrasted against Nadia's like custard drooling over gravel.

'Do I have any choice?' The thought of climbing inside the thing with Drew pressed against her bare flesh sparked the tingle again and, when he wasn't looking, Nadia gave herself a little stroke between the legs for reassurance. Being reckless once couldn't hurt, surely?

Drew needed no further encouragement. While Nadia's back was turned, he removed his T-shirt and pants but decided that he would never get the woman into the tunnel if he removed his shorts too. That, he hoped, would come later.

'It'll be easier getting into the inflatable with skin on skin. Less friction.'

Nadia's shock, when she saw his naked torso, was allayed by this justification at least until he gripped her around the waist and posted her legs through the tube. It was like trying to get into a sleeping bag underwater, especially as Nadia wasn't concentrating properly. Her attention was focused on the expanding package buried within Drew's shorts.

'To hell with this tube,' she said swatting it away. 'My face will not remain straight if we use it.'

'You mean, you won't keep a straight –' Drew stopped himself. Nadia was actually grinning and he didn't want to kill the moment. Truth be known, her silly expressions turned him on. 'What do you suggest, then?'

'Come here and I'll show you.'

To Drew's complete surprise, Nadia offered a slow wink and beckoned him to her. As he approached the Russian woman's long, lean body – the stripes of a very fit woman visible in the form of streaks of muscle stretched across her tight stomach – he became aware of the enormous erection that now strained in his shorts. How he wanted Nadia to wrap her slender fingers around his shaft and mutter something dirty in her native Russian. How he adored the power she had over him – and she didn't even know it.

'I think the researchers have been approaching this completely the wrong way,' Nadia said. 'What they don't realise, when they invent their clever contraptions, is that, when you've been in orbit for nearly ten months, you don't care how you do it. You just know you'll do it.' She pulled Drew towards her and clamped his body against the length of hers, their groins meeting again but this time with sheer lust holding them in place.

'Who needs elastic strapping and blow-up tubes?' Nadia giggled. 'Now, pretend to fuck me.'

'Affirmative, Miss Kasparova. But are you sure you just want me to pretend?' Drew began to rock his hips but, on the second shunt, Nadia floated away from him as if she were in an orbit of her own.

'That worked well,' he muttered, following her trajectory. 'We need to approach this differently. This position is obviously impossible. One of us must be stationary.'

'Fine,' Nadia said. 'Tie me up to the support brackets.' She took a moment to retrieve four cords from a locker and Drew fumbled and rushed to get her bound to the wall. 'Now I can't float away and you can grip the handles above so that you can push into me. Theoretically, of course.' She winked again.

Nadia's legs were spread wide enough for Drew to work the bulge in his shorts into the tempting mound behind the white panties. As instructed, he seized the support handles and slowly began to press his concealed cock against Nadia's knickers. When she let out a long moan, not even attempting to stifle it as she had before, and began to pulse against his movements, Drew took this as a signal that she wanted more.

'Let's make this simulation as realistic as we can.' He slipped off his shorts and began to peel

Nadia's panties down her legs. The angle of her tied legs prevented them going further than her knees, but Drew didn't care. Her desperate, love-starved pussy was only inches from his face and he took the opportunity to swivel around, so that he was inverted in relation to Nadia, and plunged his face into the depths of her sex.

Nadia yelped, partly in protestation and partly from delight as Drew's strong tongue pushed inside her. It took her a moment to realise but, in his new position, he was offering up a feast of his own. Nadia couldn't catch the buoyant erection with her tied hands so she had to seek it out with her lips and, when she did, she was rewarded with a slow and deep lick from front to back.

'Time to attempt a docking procedure, Miss Kasparova.' Drew flipped around again and pressed against Nadia's suspended body.

'Permission granted, Captain Masters.' Nadia giggled, wondering how she had survived this long without sex. Her thoughts were smothered as Drew dipped his mouth on to hers and delivered a deep kiss. She felt the tip of his cock probe the entrance to her sex and suddenly she felt like a virgin all over again.

'I shouldn't be doing this.' She pulled away, overcome by a moment of guilt as she sensed her mind and body letting go.

'Nonsense. It's for the future of mankind. One small step and all that.' Drew buried his face in

Nadia's neck and began to ease himself between the folds of her sex. Strapping her to the wall was the perfect solution. Indeed, she could be tied to the ceiling, the floor, a chair – it didn't matter as long as she was a fixed target. He planned to try each position in turn and present his findings to Mission Control. Finally, he was fully engulfed by the warmth and wetness of Nadia's pussy and as he settled into a rhythm, he wondered how he would last more than a dozen strokes.

Nadia was helpless. She had never felt so out of control – both in body and mind – and loved her newfound freedom. As she felt her orgasm approach, she rocked her hips as much as she was able and delivered squeal after squeal as pleasure ripped through her body. Unable to contain himself as he was milked by Nadia's detonation, Drew jettisoned deep inside her.

'I am sorry for yelling so much.' Nadia gasped and laughed and writhed within her straps as she caught her breath.

'We're in space,' Drew said with a smirk. He held himself close to Nadia, unwilling to separate from her smooth skin. 'No one can hear you.'

Static and several beeps suddenly filled the laboratory and the chief controller's voice came through loud and clear. 'That's not entirely true, Captain Masters. Mission Control here.'

The shocked pair frantically looked around the lab at the five cameras and, to their horror, each had a red light above the lens, indicating that they were live. Nadia began to laugh.

'Didn't you cut communications earlier?' Drew whispered.

'I must have forgotten.' Nadia was wide-eyed and a mischievous glint sparkled in the cool blue as the sun rose once again. 'But at least they've got the results they need for EROSS.'

Nadia then addressed the nearest camera and, still completely naked and tied spread-eagled to the bulkhead, she spoke to Mission Control. 'You have caught us with our pants down, sir, and my back is against the wall –' Nadia winked at Drew '– but it is all in the name of science. I am pleased to report that this particular reproductive position has been a success and we will be experimenting further over the coming days. My full report will follow but for now, suffice it to say that the world was out of this.'

With that, Drew flicked off all the cameras and turned his attentions to Nadia again. 'That'd be "out of this world",' he corrected and pulled himself level with her exposed pussy. 'Better clean up the mess before it escapes.' And he set to work.

Maya Hess is the author of the Black Lace novels *The Angels' Share* and *Bright Fire*. Her short stories have appeared in numerous Wicked Words collections.